PRAISE FOR THE NOVELS OF RUTH GLICK
(WRITING AS REBECCA YORK)

"A compulsive read."   —*Publishers Weekly*

"York delivers an exciting and suspenseful romance with paranormal themes that she gets just right. This is a howling good read."   —*Booklist*

"Mesmerizing action and passions that leap from the pages with the power of a wolf's coiled spring."
—*Bookpage*

"*Killing Moon* is a delightful supernatural private investigator romance starring two charming lead characters."
—*Midwest Book Review*

"Rebecca York delivers page-turning suspense."
—*Nora Roberts*

"Glick's prose is smooth, literate, and fast-moving; her love scenes are tender yet erotic; and there's always a happy ending."   —*The Washington Post Book World*

"A true master of intrigue."   —*Rave Reviews*

"No one sends more chills down your spine than the very creative and imaginative Ms. York!"
—*Romantic Times*

continued . . .

"She writes a fast-paced, satisfying thriller."   —UPI

"*Edge of the Moon* is clever and a great read. I can't wait to read the final book in this wonderful series."
—*Paranormal Romance Reviews*

Don't miss these other werewolf romantic suspense novels from Rebecca York

CRIMSON MOON
A young werewolf bent on protecting the environment ends up protecting a lumber baron's daughter— a woman who arouses his hunger as no other . . .

KILLING MOON
A P.I. with a preternatural talent for tracking finds his prey: a beautiful genetic researcher who may be his only hope for a future . . .

EDGE OF THE MOON
A police detective and a woman who files a missing persons report become the pawns of an unholy serial killer in a game of deadly attraction . . .

WITCHING MOON
A werewolf and a sexy biologist investigate a swamp steeped in superstition, legend, and death . . .

Baby at His Door
KATHERINE GARBERA

Silhouette®

Desire

Published by Silhouette Books
America's Publisher of Contemporary Romance

SILHOUETTE BOOKS

ISBN 0-373-76367-0

BABY AT HIS DOOR

Visit Silhouette at www.eHarlequin.com

Printed in U.S.A.

Books by Katherine Garbera

Silhouette Desire

The Bachelor Next Door #1104
Miranda's Outlaw #1169
Her Baby's Father #1289
Overnight Cinderella #1348
Baby at His Door #1367

KATHERINE GARBERA

This story is set in rural Florida, a place Katherine Garbera knows well. She grew up on different ranches in south central Florida, producing crops of oranges and gathering eggs. "There is so much more to Florida than most people even realize." The fictional town of Placid Springs is based very loosely on the city of Okeechobee, where her grandparents lived. Katherine is a member of Romance Writers of America, Novelists, Inc. and the Authors Guild.

This book is dedicated to Kathy and Ed Garbera.
Thanks for raising the wonderful man
who is my husband and for welcoming me
into your family as a daughter, not a daughter-in-law.

Acknowledgments:
Thanks to Kelley Pounds, who answered my questions
on ranching and for being a good enough friend that a
couple pages of questions didn't intimidate her!
Any errors are my own.

The clerical team at DEP has been an endless source of
support and friendship for me in the last five years,
and I want to thank them all. Being a secretary isn't
always a glamour job, and these women helped me
do a thankless job with grace and laughter.

Thanks also to my family
for their unending support and love.

And lastly, thanks to Ann Leslie Tuttle
for her insight and wisdom.

One

Evan Powell cursed whatever fate made the doorbell ring when he'd just stepped out of the shower. Working two jobs consumed all of his time and energy. He'd just finished his martial arts workout and relaxing afterward was the only part of his endless day he savored.

The doorbell pealed again. He wanted to get it before his dad woke. Damn.

Wrapping a large brown towel around his waist, he glimpsed his own visage in the mirror. He looked like a harsh man. The kind of man who'd lived a hard life. He knew the mirror didn't lie. If anything it softened his image.

He hoped to God one of his deputies was ringing

the bell. Maybe Hobbs, his newest recruit, who was still wet behind the ears. A neighbor or tourist would probably run for the hills, seeing him. Except Florida didn't have hills, he thought.

He stalked through the dark house. The grandfather clock in the hall chimed one o'clock. If his favorite cow hadn't chosen tonight to give birth he'd already be in bed and resting. Only an emergency would bring someone out at this time of night.

He should take time to grab some pants, he thought. But he wasn't feeling hospitable and didn't really feel like making the effort of dressing. He paused by the locked gun cabinet in the living room to grab his weapon. The .45 felt right in his hand, something he never examined too closely.

Pants were an option but his gun wasn't. When had life been brought down to survive or die? he wondered. He knew it had a lot to do with the training he'd received in Quantico.

He flicked on the porch light, then swung the door open, hiding the gun behind the barrier of wood and glass. A slender woman with slicked-back blond hair stood in the doorway. A gash on her head bled slowly, and her deep blue eyes were wide with shock.

"I wrecked my car," she said. Her voice had a slightly high pitch and no accent. She wavered on her feet, and he reached out to steady her. The feel of expensive silk beneath his fingers was foreign. For a moment he wanted to enjoy the sensation of caressing luxury, but he couldn't. People who stared through shop windows at things they couldn't have only ended up drooling on themselves.

"Where?" he asked, reminding himself he was the sheriff and had sworn to protect and serve civilians.

She gestured wildly toward the long, winding driveway and the highway. Had she walked from the wreck? She had to be exhausted.

The harsh fluorescent lamp was punishing, revealing her shock and fatigue in stark detail. Her skin looked so fine it seemed almost translucent. He wanted to touch her. Her flesh couldn't be as soft as it looked. Annoyed, he realized she aroused him. He must be more tired than he thought if this woman was slipping past his guard.

She should have appeared chic and sophisticated, if her clothes and haircut were any indication, and to some extent she did. But there was an air of fragility and innocence about her. Not the debauched boredom that he'd encountered countless times in the rich.

Those emotions were oddly out of step with what he expected of her type. His ex-wife Shanna had the same sleek look about her but absolutely no fragility or innocence. In fact, Shanna was a barracuda, swimming through the masses of men who thronged around her in search of a weak one to kill.

"Where's your car?" he repeated.

"At the edge of your property, at least I think it's your property. Do you own the Rockin' PJP Ranch? There was a cow and a..." Her voice trailed off as her gaze swept down his body, and she realized he wore only a towel.

When her eyes widened, he saw a hint of female speculation in her gaze before fear entered. She struggled to free herself, pulling frantically on her arm. He set his gun on the hall table. He held her shoulders in both of his hands, afraid she'd fall down the porch steps and further injure herself in her frantic bid for escape.

"Hold still, dammit. I'm not going to hurt you." It was odd that he had to reassure her. Being the local law meant that most people turned to him for protection. Though he knew the lack of a uniform probably had a lot to do with her reaction. He wasn't a safe-looking guy. He was a tough hombre, he thought, remembering his wisecracking deputy's description.

Still, damn few people ran from him. If they did, they had a reason. This little lady sure didn't have anything to fear from him.

She aimed him a haughty look, bringing the poise and elegance he'd only speculated about earlier to the fore.

Evan released her and spread his hands wide. "I'm the sheriff."

"Where's your badge? And no, I don't want to see your stick."

Evan bit back the laughter rising in his throat. He liked this feisty woman even though she'd disturbed his peaceful night.

He wanted to touch her again. To see if she reacted

as quickly to passion as she did to anger. He wished he'd slid his palms down her arms before he'd released her. He'd bet his next month's pay she'd be soft and smooth. She had that pampered look.

"Don't run off. I'll go get my pants and my badge, and we'll go see about your car."

"Okay," she said, her body relaxing. The shocked expression left her and a tentative half-grin lit her face.

"Do you want to wait inside or would you feel safer on the porch?" he asked.

"I'll wait out here."

He couldn't blame her. Though he knew he meant her no harm, she had to trust and depend on herself for protection until he proved himself harmless.

"We've got two dogs who have the run of the place so if they show up while I'm gone don't be alarmed. They're all bark," he said as he headed for the stairs.

"Like their owner," she muttered.

Though he knew her words hadn't been intended to reach him, he pivoted and walked back toward her. "I'm not all bark."

She held her spine stiff and straight in a way that reminded him of a proud twenty-year Marine. When she spoke, the sparkle in her eye reassured him her injury wasn't too serious. "I didn't say you were."

He reached out with his free hand brushing a finger down the side of her cheek. Dammit, she was as soft as he'd suspected. "Sure you did, sweetheart. You just hoped I wouldn't hear."

He backed away, knowing if he stayed too close

he'd be tempted.... Tempted to touch her again with his mouth. Tempted to pull her soft curvy body into the hard muscles of his. Tempted to forget his good sense and take what her snapping eyes didn't know they offered.

"If I didn't want you to hear, I wouldn't have said it out loud."

He liked her grit. "I'm your only hope of not standing outside all night, so you might want to remember that."

"I will. I'm sorry. I'm just tired and scared."

Evan softened toward her. She seemed delicate and he wanted to comfort her. How many times did he have to learn the same lesson? Although he was torn, he knew better.

Women weren't the weaker sex, as men had stupidly assumed for eons. They were a powerhouse. And no one knew that better than Evan Powell.

"It's okay. I do resemble the dogs in some ways."

"Which ways?" she asked, her eyes alight with curiosity instead of shock.

I'm loyal and trustworthy, he thought. But didn't say it out loud because it would leave him vulnerable. "I'll let you figure it out."

He turned to go, knowing he shouldn't make a parting comment, but he couldn't help himself. "By the way, sweetheart. I don't show my *stick* to just anyone."

Evan left her out in the night air but didn't close the door. She might change her mind about coming inside once he left. He took his gun with him, locking it back in the cabinet before going upstairs to dress. He never left his guns unlocked.

He thought about the woman waiting for him on his front porch. She screamed big city. The kind of lady he knew better than to tangle with, yet part of him wanted to do just that. He wanted to take care of her wound, then comfort her in his arms.

Dammit, old son, haven't you already learned that lesson? He didn't answer himself.

Lydia couldn't believe she stood on the porch of some backwoods sheriff's house. Florida was surprisingly cold on this May night and frightening. Foreign noises grew in volume in the darkness, and she couldn't hear a single car honking or taxi driver cursing. This remote place was nothing like her aunt's place farther south in Deerfield Beach.

But it wasn't all an unpleasant experience. The scent of orange blossoms filled the air, and the full moon painted pretty shadow pictures on the ground. Taking a deep breath, she stared up at the sky.

She shivered and ran her hands over her bare arms. Her short-sleeved designer pantsuit might look nice indoors, but outside it offered no protection. Expensive but worthless. Like her?

That line of thinking was too depressing to pursue. Her car was wrecked. She couldn't give her name or any other information to the cops. They'd call her father, and she couldn't go home. At least not yet.

After the accident, she'd listened to the warning bell telling her the car door was ajar, realizing that something inside her was ajar. She couldn't go back home. She couldn't continue on to Aunt Gracie's house either because her car was totaled. The future was already written in stone, and it looked long and lonely from where she sat.

She'd have to wing it. But she wasn't good at spur-of-the-moment things. The last time she'd tried to be spontaneous she'd discovered her fiancé in bed with his mistress. No, she thought, don't go there.

She hadn't loved Paul Draper but she'd liked him and thought they'd have a chance at a decent sort of marriage. But Paul hadn't believed in commitment to one woman, especially a wife.

Catching Paul in bed with another woman hadn't broken her heart, but it had made her think about marrying for any reason other than love. She'd quietly left Paul's apartment and informed her father that she wasn't rushing into marriage. For the first time he'd gotten truly angry with her and insisted she would marry Paul. Feeling trapped Lydia had escaped in the middle of the night with no clear plan of where she was going—only knowing she couldn't stay in New York City.

She'd looked into the darkening night and made a desperate decision to change the course of her fate. She was going to have to be in the driver's seat if she didn't want to take that long, lonely walk down the marriage aisle in September. She had this summer.

One short summer to find an alternative and to find *herself* before she had to make a decision to either submit to her father's vision of her destiny or change her life forever. During the long walk to the ranch house she'd vacillated, not coming up with any solution, but one thing had been clear—her determination not to play the role her father had chosen for her.

She'd always been close to her father, and they'd grown closer in the last ten years since her mother's death. Close enough for her to have been fooled by him when he said that she should marry for love and not position.

She was the child of an illicit affair and had lived in a posh Manhattan penthouse with both of her parents all her life, even though they'd never married. She'd gone to an exclusive boarding school with children of rock stars and politicians so her parents not being married had never been an issue. Actually, her family had been closer to normal than any.

Her father would drag her back home, and she'd be forced to marry Paul. She would have thought her father had enough respect for her at twenty-five to let her make her own decisions. But no.

Two months ago he'd come home from the office and announced that she should be married in six months. He'd asked if she had any prospects. Thinking he was joking she'd said no, she was going to be an old maid.

From that moment on her father had shoved one single executive after another down her throat. She'd been on more blind dates and accidental dinners than she'd ever wanted. And it had soon become clear that these men weren't interested in her as anything other than the means to an end.

She wanted to find her Prince Charming and be swept off her feet by him. She'd come to realize that in real life the handsome, wealthy prince might not be the greatest catch. He might be self-absorbed and cold. Her real-life, handsome, wealthy prince would certainly never banter with her.

She didn't want to be married off for her position in society, to a man who saw her only as a bank account, she thought sadly. It made her wonder what, if anything, Paul wanted from her. He was her father's second in command at work. He really had nothing to gain by marrying her. Except a lot of money.

Oh, great. She was getting maudlin. She was too young and spunky to be so melodramatic, she reminded herself. But the lesson didn't sink in. Tonight, she was tired and cold and her head ached. Taking a deep breath, she sank down onto one of the porch steps. She wanted to bury her face in her hands, but the wound on her head prohibited that. So she rested her chin on her up-drawn legs.

When the good-looking sheriff came back she was going to have to lie for all she was worth to convince him she was nothing more than she appeared. A down-on-her-luck-lady.

She loved her dad, but she wasn't ready to go back to Manhattan yet. He was too steely-eyed in his determination for her to marry Paul. She'd left him a note with a brief admonition not to worry, but she knew him. Martin Kerr wasn't going to let her stay hidden.

She wondered if the sheriff would believe she had amnesia? She doubted it. Besides, on the soaps, amnesia victims were always immediately unsure of where they were and what they were doing. She'd probably blown her chance. Frankly, she didn't know if she was up to inventing a complicated lie.

Simplicity seemed her smartest route. She'd already removed her license plate and hidden it in her suitcase so they couldn't trace the car to her New York address. She'd also left her cell phone behind, knowing she'd answer it if her dad called and she needed distance to think. She'd have to make up a name and a story. A good one because, even though this was a small-town sheriff, keen intelligence had gleamed in his eyes. Also a predatory awareness that she'd rarely encountered in men. He wasn't going to be distracted by batting eyelashes and fingers stroking down his arm.

She liked the sheriff. Liked the lean body she'd observed while he'd talked with her. Liked the line of hair that tapered down his washboard stomach beneath the line of the brown towel. Liked the easy strength he'd used to hold her with when she'd tried to escape. Liked especially the fact that he hadn't hurt her.

She heard feet pounding the earth, and a minute later two monsters surrounded her. Dogs were cute fluffy white things with pink or yellow bows in their hair. These dirty phantoms wanted to eat her alive, she realized as wet coarse tongues swept over her arms and face.

She screamed and tried to scramble to her feet. A strong hand grabbed her upper arm, steadying her. Grateful for the sheriff's assistance she clung to him. She felt tears burn the back of her eyes and felt not only the helplessness of her current situation, but also the weight of her life and the decision she'd made.

"Settle down, boys," the sheriff ordered, appearing by her side.

The dogs stilled and then, after a hand movement from the sheriff, disappeared around the corner. Lydia could hardly contain her breathing. The sheriff ran a soothing hand down her spine.

"So you don't like dogs?" he asked, in a laconic drawl that made her want to kick him.

"I like show dogs. Pets with manners," she said. To her own ears her voice sounded thin and airy. Did she sound that weak to him?

"Those are real dogs for real men, sweetheart. Not the cultured kind of pet you find in the city."

"How did you know I'm from the city?" she asked. Oh, God, did he know who she was? For the first time since he'd rejoined her, she studied him.

Her breath caught in her throat. If he'd been sexy wearing only a towel, he was even more so clothed in a black T-shirt and faded jeans. She liked the smile in his eyes and the quiet confidence he projected. She didn't want to like him because she had to deceive him, but she knew there was little hope for resisting him.

He shrugged his shoulder and scratched his chin before answering her. "You just have the look of the city."

He had no idea how right he was. She did have *the look*, had, in fact, been part of a national campaign with her supermodel mother when she was fifteen. Lydia bit her lip as thoughts of her mother assailed her. Her mother had been killed in the terrorist downing of a plane.

"I didn't realize bloody wounds and rumpled clothing were in fashion this year," she quipped.

"Maybe you'll start a trend."

She doubted it. She hated the spotlight. Uncomfortable with the silence between them, she diverted the conversation to business. "I should have asked you for a phone earlier to call a wrecker."

"I already took care of that. And I've called one of my deputies and an ambulance. They'll be waiting for us by your car. Here's my badge, by the way," he said, quickly extending the badge for her to see. "Come on, I'll give you a ride back to your vehicle."

"Thanks."

She'd always had everything she wanted but riding in a 4X4 would be a new experience. If she'd walked back to her car, her feet would have protested. His big truck sported a little step built under the door. Thank God, she thought. Otherwise she wouldn't have been able to climb inside without help.

The sheriff stood behind her anyway and boosted her to the step. She seated herself, then realized they were eye-to-eye. He was a tall man, this sheriff. His eyes were an icy gray. The play of light over his features fascinated her. A strong jaw and sun and laugh lines that radiated outward from his eyes.

A real man. A shiver of awareness spread through her body and pooled at her center. She'd bet her last hundred-dollar bill that he had the kind of muscles you couldn't get with weekly trips to the fitness center. Stop it, she warned herself.

She'd never been on her own, and the prospect was daunting. For a moment she wanted to return to the familiar, her prestigious name and large bank account. But she also wanted the chance to prove to herself that she was more than a commodity to be sold to the highest bidder.

"Thank you, sir."

"I'm Evan Powell. Please call me Evan," he said.

"Thank you, Evan."

"You're welcome...."

He wanted to know her name. Come on girl, think. The safest name would be her own. She'd use her middle name, which was what her closest friends called her anyway. She'd give her father's name for the last name. "Lydia Martin."

"Lydia," he repeated her name as if savoring the feel of it on his tongue.

He closed the door. She watched him walk around the truck and sucked in a few deep breaths before he returned. The cab smelled warm and masculine. Like his aftershave, she realized as he climbed behind the wheel.

He started the truck and the twang of country guitar filled it. He reached out to turn down the volume and she watched his hands. Twice he'd held her arm. She wondered what his touch would feel like in a different context and not on her arm. Her nipples tightened against her lacy bra.

"Are you visiting around these parts?" he asked.

Glad for the distraction from her thoughts, she said, "No, I'm just passing through. I was heading to Deerfield Beach to stay with my aunt."

They'd reached the end of his driveway. "Which way?"

"Left."

Her BMW was still wrapped around a telephone pole, and the wreck looked a lot worse in the harsh light cast by his 4X4 truck. "I'm surprised you were able to walk away."

"The air bag and seat belt saved my life," she said and knew it was true.

Amazing she'd survived, she thought as she stared at the twisted pile of metal. She felt as if she'd been given another chance at life, and she decided to make the most of it. If she wanted to marry for love she'd have to find a man worthy of her love—and find out if she was worthy of his love. The ideas she'd been playing with earlier solidified, and she knew a sense of purpose for the first time in her life. And that pur-

pose was going to take her in the opposite direction
to where her life had been heading.

The police, ambulance and wrecker all arrived while
she watched from the cab of Evan's truck. She felt a
little like a fairy-tale princess who'd just been awakened from a long sleep. Only this princess would
travel a harder road to find her knight in shining armor
and live happily ever after.

Two

It was bad enough Evan was attracted to a tourist he was sworn to protect and serve but to discover one of his cows had caused the accident was a fitting end to the night. Lydia, who'd yet to produce an ID, didn't want to press charges. But Evan knew he'd have to cover the car repair and probably a couple of nights' motel stay.

Though the EMT who examined her feared she might have a concussion, she refused to go to the hospital and stay overnight. Evan knew he couldn't dump her in a motel.

"She can stay with me tonight," he volunteered.

The EMT gave him instructions to wake her every two hours and ask her a few questions.

"I don't want to be an imposition," Lydia said after the EMT had left.

"You won't be. I take in boarders in the summer."

"Really, I'll be fine in a motel."

"It's either my place or the hospital, sweetheart."

"Listen here, Sheriff. I don't take orders from anyone."

"I'm not giving you an order. I'm making a decision for you. You are too impaired due to your injury to decide on your own."

She glared at him. He'd love to see her rested and at her full fighting strength. "I'm not going to the hospital."

"Then I'd love to have you as my guest."

"You're not going to offer to show me your stick are you?"

Evan laughed. "No, not yet."

He spared a few minutes to radio his foreman to come get the cow back inside the fence. Then have his men repair the broken section. It had been a long time since he'd met a woman he could spar with verbally. Most of the hometown girls never stood up to him. He caught up with Lydia arguing with the tow-truck driver, Boz Stillman.

"Listen, lady. It's going to take weeks—two, maybe three, to repair your car. Why don't you just let me take it to the junkyard and have your insurance carrier reimburse you?" Boz demanded.

"The car is still in working condition. I don't want it totaled," Lydia said.

"Do you have insurance?" Evan asked. Her insistence about repairing her car told him she might not be covered. He glanced toward the car and found Boz's helper unloading a fortune's worth of designer luggage from the trunk.

"No," she said, quietly.

"Boz, tow the car in and make the repairs to it."

"Um…Evan, may I speak with you for a minute?" Lydia asked. Her voice was soft and sweet, not a bit at odds with the woman who'd clung to him when his dogs had been licking her.

"Sure. Give us a minute, Boz."

Boz walked away mumbling about women with more looks than sense. Lydia shifted her weight from foot to foot and stared off at the red-and-blue flashing lights of the squad car.

"What did you want to discuss?"

"This is kind of hard to say," Lydia hedged.

"Spit it out," he said, unable to believe she had trouble saying what was on her mind.

"I don't have any money right now."

"Don't you have credit cards?" She seemed like the type who'd have a wallet full of gold cards.

"No. I don't like to use them," she said, staring at the ground.

"Let me pay for the repairs. It's the least I can do since my cow caused the accident."

"No. You're already paying me back by letting me stay at your house tonight. Maybe I can find a job and earn some cash to pay for the repairs. This car looks like it's going to take some time to fix.''

"I'll pay Boz for the repairs when he's finished and then you can send me a check from your relative's house when you get there.''

"My aunt is out of town. I'm house-sitting for her.''

Of course, he thought. Because he'd been thinking that he could spar with her and enjoy the tinges of arousal racing through his veins until she left, it looked like she was going to have to stay.

"What's your career?''

"I don't have one. I do a lot of work with charities.''

Great, no marketable skills. He sighed. She appealed to him, he should be getting farther away from her, but instead...

"I have some filing that needs to be done at the office. You can work for me until your car is ready. I'll pay for your repairs and give you room and board. Sound good?''

"Don't you have to get some sort of approval for that?''

Yes, but that was his worry not hers. "Don't you ever stop arguing?''

She grinned at him, looking like an impish fairy for a brief moment. "No, I don't.''

"Somehow I suspected that.''

"I really appreciate all you're doing for me.''

"No problem. Let me get your luggage loaded in the back of the truck and we'll head home.''

"Don't you need to stay here?"

"Nah, my deputy needs the experience of writing up paperwork."

Despite her evasive answers, he wanted her like hell on fire. Damn, he should have let her go to the motel, but he couldn't let her stay in a lonely motel room. As ridiculous as it seemed, he wanted to watch over her while she slept.

Lydia woke in a dark room. The deep and steady sound of someone else's breathing alarmed her. Where was she?

The window was open and the curtain billowed gently in the breeze. There were foreign sounds, cicadas, grasshoppers and the lowing of cows filling the air. Not like Manhattan.

The pillow beneath her head was firm, not the cloud-like softness of her own goose-down pillow. The sheets were cotton, and she seemed to be wearing some sort of sleep shirt with buttons.

She sat up, trying to identify the other person in the room. A familiar scent assailed her. Woodsy and masculine. An aftershave that was familiar to her but not her father's.

"Lydia? Are you awake?"

The sheriff, Evan. The events of the night rushed back to her. She'd been in a wreck and instead of doing the smart thing and telling the truth, she'd concocted a story to cover herself. And not much of one at that.

For the first time since her father had made public his intention to buy her a husband six months ago she felt free.

She shrugged aside the feelings of melancholy and vulnerability and savored instead her newfound freedom.

The neon glow of the clock on the nightstand said six-fifteen. The second time she'd wakened, she thought. The first time he'd awakened her, and it had been vague and annoying because she was so tired.

This man wanted nothing from her. He didn't care that she had a large sum of money tied to her. His concern for her safety came from the genuine goodness inside him. He was a tough-looking character, but he had a good heart. She'd noticed that not only in the way he'd dealt with her, but also in how he interacted with the other professionals at the accident scene.

"Yes, Sheriff, I am."

He made a tsking sound and walked over to the bed. A click and then the bedside light was on. "I thought we agreed you'd call me Evan?"

He looked rumpled and sleepy, and she wanted to open her arms, pull back the covers and invite him to rest his weary body next to hers. Some deep primal instinct made her want to comfort him. "You're right—Evan."

"That's better," he said, caressing her cheek.

His touch sent shivers of awareness coursing through her veins. The electric pulses were the forerunners of desire, Lydia thought, with no small shock.

She'd never felt desire before this evening. Never wanted a man to linger when he caressed or kissed her. She enjoyed the touch and resented its loss when Evan pulled back.

"I'm going to have to head out soon to start the morning chores before going into town. You can take today off and start that job at the office tomorrow. My father will wake you in two hours to make sure you don't have a concussion."

He liked to give orders, Lydia realized.

"Yes, sir," she said, with a tinge of disrespect.

"Does your mouth ever get you into trouble?" he asked.

"Not anything I can't handle," she said, feeling flirty from his touch. Would he caress her again if she sat up? Could she tempt him into kissing her?

She sat, letting the top sheet drop to her waist. His gaze skimmed down her body lingering over the curve of her breast before he looked away.

"I'm sure," he said, walking to the door.

"Evan."

He glanced back over his shoulder; cloaked as he was in the shadows spilling from the opening doorway, his expression was inscrutable.

"Sorry."

He crossed back to her, taking her shoulders in his hands, he leaned her back against the pillow. He pulled the sheet up to her neck, and his hands lingered on her body. She wanted to wriggle around and bring his touch closer to the aching parts of her body.

"Don't tease me, Lydia. I'll take what you're offering and give you back passion like you've never found before."

"I wasn't teasing."

"What were you doing?"

"I don't know. But your touch…"

"Yes?"

"Your touch is like the sweetest imported chocolate I've ever had. One that I savored for months, coming back time and again for a tiny lick. I wanted one more lick."

"Not right now," he said.

"No, not right now," she agreed.

He walked to the door again. Just as he stepped into the hallway, she leaned up on her elbow. "Evan, I don't think I'll be satisfied with just one lick."

"Neither will I," he said and disappeared.

"There's a woman in the house."

Evan didn't look up from putting his tack away. "Yes, Dad, there is."

"Why?" Payne asked.

"She had a wreck last night avoiding one of our cows." Evan closed the tack-room door and started up toward the house. His father fell into step beside him. Evan watched the old man from the corner of his eye. He wondered if Payne ever got lonely living out here with just Evan and ranch hands for company.

"We've got insurance," Payne said, interrupting his thoughts.

Evan nodded. "She has a head injury."

"Concussion?" Payne asked as they entered the kitchen. Both men stopped to kick off their boots. One of Evan's mother's lingering edicts. No dirty boots in the house. She'd been dead for over twenty years, but they still wouldn't track muck into her kitchen.

"I don't think so. But we couldn't be sure."

"That's good. When's she leaving?"

"She's broke. I'm going to put her to work at the sheriff's office until she has enough money to pay off her car."

"Do you know what you're doing, son?"

Evan nodded.

"She looks a little like Shanna."

"I know."

"See that you remember that."

Evan started breakfast trying to forget what his father's words meant.

Shanna had been spoiled, and though she'd loved him at school, his hometown had been too much for her. She'd begged him to move back to D.C. with her. To go back to working with the FBI when it became apparent that ranch life wasn't what she'd envisioned. But he hadn't loved her enough to leave his family and his home. Nor had she.

He'd been a mess when Shanna had left him for the bright lights of D.C. But Evan had learned that lesson. He didn't need a reminder. Fooling around with Lydia was all he had in mind. And that was more dreaming than anything else. If she stayed here, there were Payne and a dozen ranch hands to act as chaperones.

The two Powell men sat down to a cold cereal breakfast without speaking. The silence was comfortable to them and they both enjoyed it for their own reasons.

The phone interrupted breakfast, and Payne, closest to the wall unit, reached out his long arm to answer it. He nodded to Evan. Evan took the call in the other room.

"What's up, Hobbs?"

"I ran the description of the car and the lady last night and nothing came up."

"Okay, we'll look into it when I come down this afternoon."

Lydia passed by the doorway as Evan hung up the phone. "Lydia?"

"Yes?" she said.

He saw that the lights last night hadn't fooled him, she was even more beautiful in the pure light of day. Her icy blond hair was pulled into a chignon. He knew it wasn't a bun because his mother had explained women's hairstyles to him when he was a boy.

"We couldn't find your name in the computer last night to match to the car. I'm going to need you to write down the spelling."

She hesitated a second before she looked away. "Okay."

"Is this going to be a problem?"

Her face was transparent and her eyes, which were

a deep sapphire this morning, wouldn't meet his. She wore a stylish sundress with thin straps and a short skirt. She had knockout legs. He longed to feel them wrapped around his hips.

Dammit, get your mind back to business. The wound on her forehead had disappeared. She had a good hand with makeup, he thought.

"No. It's just that well...the car isn't registered in my name." She was lying to him. And she wasn't very good at it.

"You know we can find out who you are from the vehicle identification number, right?"

"Really?"

He nodded.

She moved closer to him. Her expensive perfume surrounded him, and he could think of nothing but searching her body to find out where she'd dabbed it. "Will you take my word for it that I haven't done anything illegal and the car really is mine?"

She had innocent eyes; he didn't think she'd done anything illegal. There was something about the eyes of a criminal that you never forgot. "Maybe."

"Maybe? What would it take to make that a yes?" she asked, moving a breath closer and running her finger along his jaw.

"More than a lick," he said stepping away. Damn, he liked flirting with a sassy woman. He hadn't realized how much he missed it until this very moment. If he stayed in the room with her alone for a few more seconds he was going to forget his good sense and kiss her. Take those perfectly painted lips beneath his own and not come up for air until she forgot about the stories she was trying to tell him.

"Well that's all I've got to offer right now," she said.

"Let's go have some breakfast and you can meet my dad. You can tell me the details of why you're using an assumed name on the way into town."

He followed her down the hall to the silence of the kitchen, watching her hips sway with each step and feeling arousal tingle along his spine and groin. He wanted her, and she had to know. He'd always been transparent when he was in lust.

He was once again in the crossfire that had cut him down before. A lying woman he wanted more than his next breath or his job. He'd chosen poorly the first time. He wouldn't again.

Three

Staying in the small town of Placid Springs, Florida, was going to be an experience. To call it a town was being generous. The one main street possessed a flashing caution signal, and there wasn't a department store to be found.

She'd come into the office with Evan because she couldn't stand being alone with her thoughts. The sheriff's office was besieged by well-wishers and curiosity seekers for a good part of the afternoon while she was there. Every person in the small town knew each other. Apparently she was the first person to hit a light pole while avoiding a cow.

"Most people just stop, ma'am. The cows rarely ram ya'," one old-timer told her.

She was between a rock and a hard place. Evan embodied all of the qualities she'd found lacking in the men she'd dated. And after meeting the kind older gentleman that was Evan's father, she doubted Evan would understand how demanding a father could be.

The mechanic had called; it was going to take two weeks for the parts needed to repair her car to come in. She wished Aunt Gracie was home so she could wire her some money. No, she didn't, she wanted to do this on her own.

Say it again, she thought, maybe you'll begin to believe it.

"We still can't find your name in our computers."

Lydia flinched and stared up into the sheriff's frozen gray eyes. She'd tried to think of how to get around having her father find out where she was while still assuaging the local law-enforcement needs. "I..."

"Yes?" he drawled.

She buried her face in her hands. Damn, she wasn't a good liar, never had been.

The warm hand on her shoulder told her Evan had moved. Tingles spread down from her shoulder, for a moment his touch made her feel safe and secure. *Tell me your secrets.*

She'd made a second chance for herself, and only she could determine if it would be a life made of lies or truth. Taking a deep breath, she looked up at him. The sexy small-town sheriff. "My name's not going to be in your computer."

His eyes narrowed, but his tone was calm. "Why not?"

"Because I haven't given you my real one."

"Why not?"

"I'm hiding and I'm not ready to be found yet."

"From whom?"

"I'd rather not say right now."

"I'm afraid I'm going to have to insist."

"Oh."

"Yes, oh."

Lydia didn't want to lie. Instead she batted her eyelashes and brushed her tongue across her bottom lip. His eyes tracked the movement like a spy satellite tracking fleet movements. She leaned forward and shrugged her shoulders until the V of her blouse dipped lower.

"Honey..."

"Yes," she said, trying to sound sultry.

"Even if I take you up on your invitation, I'm still going to want answers."

If he took her up on her invitation, she'd go down fast. One fiancé hadn't given her enough experience to handle this man and his earthy sensuality.

"I wasn't issuing an invitation per se."

"What were you doing?"

"Distracting you."

"It almost worked."

"What would it take to be successful?"

He leaned down until his breath brushed her face and she could see the flecks of sapphire in his gray eyes. She wanted to scoot away from him. Every survival instinct she had screamed for her to retreat, but this was the new Lydia and she wasn't backing up.

"More than lust, less than love."

His words cut through her. All men wanted less than love. "I'm not any good at lust."

"Hell, honey, you were doing just fine."

She shrugged.

"Ready to tell me more?"

"Not now. Can I have a reprieve?"

He nodded. "Until tonight."

"Agreed, tonight. Where will I be working?"

"Come on. I'll show you."

She followed him down the hall, noticing the fit of his uniform pants was close to illegal. He had a nice butt. She wondered if his flesh would be rock-hard, like the muscles of his naked chest had been last night. Her fingers tingled with the need to caress him again. Though this time with intent and purpose.

"Your desk will be here," he gestured to a battered model covered in manila folders and sloppily stacked papers.

The real world was a messy one, she realized. "I don't think I'll be here long enough to get through all of this paperwork."

"It looks worse than it is."

"That's what you said about the dogs."

He gave her a sympathetic look. Silence grew between them. She should stop looking at his mouth and wondering how well he kissed—spectacularly, if the darkly arousing secrets in his eyes were any indication. He had firm-looking lips. Kind of went with the rest of his hard body. She wondered what his mouth would feel like on hers.

Would he kiss with restraint as her fiancé had? Or with passion?

But he was out of her league. *More than lust and less than love* was not what she was looking for from a man.

"Penny for your thoughts?" he said.

Darn it. What was she going to say? The old Lydia had a stock of ditzy answers that made everyone around her think she was a shallow socialite. But last night she'd had a blinding realization that life held more for her than an arranged marriage and it was up to her to find it. It was time to leave the ditz behind.

"I was thinking about you," she said, before her courage could desert her.

"What about me?" he asked, taking a step closer. The sounds of the common room just outside this little office cubicle suddenly seemed a world away. His shoulders blocked the entrance, nearly spanning it.

He was a big man, she thought. Big and strong and honest as the day is long. Though she longed to feel his arms around her, she knew she never would. This was a man who would not tolerate lies, especially from someone he'd been intimate with. That made her a little sad.

The thought shocked her because she hadn't realized how much she wanted him until that moment.

Lust was a new emotion to her, and she wasn't sure she liked it.

"Lydia?"

She glanced up, meeting his icy gaze. She should hedge and lie. No, she thought fiercely. Not about this, not about the feelings he evoked in her. She'd stick to the truth about everything except her identity.

"What were you thinking?" he queried again.

Taking a deep breath she told him the truth for the first time since they met. "I was wondering what your mouth would feel like on my own. And then I remembered lust not love."

He froze. Obviously not expecting honesty from someone who was feeding him half lies the way a con man sells security. He cocked his head to the side and stepped forward, moving with surety and grace. No tentative steps such as she would have used.

She felt the warmth of his body before he came close enough for his chest to brush her breasts. She tilted her head to look up at him. His silver-gray eyes were narrowed and those firm hard lips were parted.

She felt the exhalation of his breath as he leaned forward. Smelled the coffee he'd drunk earlier while she'd been on the phone. Closing her eyes she let her senses absorb every sensation of the moment.

"Lydia?" he asked, his voice a husky rasp.

She opened her eyes and saw in his gaze intent. Though he didn't speak, she knew he'd wondered what it would be like to kiss her. Her, a woman with no money or power tied to her. *Just an average woman.* Her heartbeat sped up and she lifted her hands to his shoulders.

The cotton of his uniform, starched to perfection, was a new texture. She slid her fingers across the fabric, feeling the strength of the man before her. This wasn't a man who'd allow himself to be purchased.

This was a man who lived life by his own rules. And as his head lowered slowly toward hers, she realized this was a man who could teach her more of life than just the passionate side she'd never experienced. By example he could teach her how to carve her own niche in the world.

She stood on her toes to reach his lips as they descended. Losing her balance, she fell forward, her breasts brushing his chest. Her nipples tightened and her blood seemed heavier as it flowed through her veins.

He angled his head, she closed her eyes.

"Sheriff?"

"Dammit."

He pivoted to face the open doorway. Lydia drew her hands down and laced her fingers together.

"Phone," one of his deputies said. Evan ran a hand through his hair and walked away without looking back at her. What had almost happened?

Lydia leaned against the edge of the cluttered desk and wrapped her arms around her waist. Her heart was racing, her blood pounding and her most feminine parts were crying out for more of that man. Evan Powell made her feel alive. She realized she was staying in Placid Springs for more than a desire to earn her own way. She wanted to spend more time with the sheriff.

A warm breeze blew through the open windows of the cab of Evan's truck. Lydia stared out the window as if the view held the secrets to the universe. She had been pensive and withdrawn since their conversation this afternoon. He wondered what she was hiding from.

She had the pampered look of a rich wife. Which gave him pause. No matter how much he wanted her or she flirted with him he wasn't poaching in another man's territory.

He'd never questioned his control. It had been his constant companion since his ex-wife's desertion. But even rock-solid control and the possibility that Lydia might be married wasn't enough to keep him from wanting to reach out and touch the slim thighs revealed by her skirt.

Lydia's soft voice as she sang along with the radio played along his senses, with the warm breeze and earthy scents setting off longings he had no right to. He wanted to pull the truck off the road and revel in his senses. To fill them until he was drunk on the sensations of woman, world and endless time.

Dammit, Lydia called to his soul the way D.C. had called to his secret hidden dreams. She represented everything about the world outside of Placid Springs that he wanted but didn't have. Everyone in the small town had stopped by to see her and talk to her about the cow accident. *Did you see the pretty lady in Evan's office?*

The lady didn't belong with him any more than she did this small town. But he wanted her.

Damn, he wished he'd never thought of kissing her. But since he had, his mind kept supplying him with images and imagined textures. Images of her straddling his hips, her skirt floating over his thighs while she rode him to completion. The imagined texture of her skin and her mouth. The soft wet, living silk of female.

"Evan?"

Forcing his concentration to the present and away from hot dreams, he glanced over at her.

"I'm sorry about those papers," she said.

She'd mixed up the fax and the shredder machines. Whatever Lydia had done in the life she was running from, she had not been a top-rate office assistant. "Don't worry about it."

"Are you going to fire me?" she asked after minutes had passed.

"I'm not."

"Are you upset about something?

"I'm not *upset*. What kind of a wimpy word is that to use on a man?"

"I don't know, Marlboro Man, why don't you tell me?"

"It was a long day," he said at last. "I like the silence."

"Are you sure that's all?"

"Yes."

"You can talk to me about your problems. I'd be happy to be your sounding board," she said, placing her hand on his thigh.

"No, thank you."

"Really. It's something I'm good at. Unless of course you don't like me."

"Look, Lydia. I like you."

"Then what's the problem?"

"You're funny and sexy and everything I like about big-city women. But you're not staying here. For us to do more than work together would be a mistake."

"I was talking about work."

He glanced pointedly to the hand resting on his thigh. "You were flirting."

Hastily she removed her touch. She laced her fingers together in her lap and owned up to the truth. "Yes I was. I thought you were interested in more than lust, less than love."

"I said that's what would have made me stop questioning you."

"Not interested?" she asked.

"You're a complication I don't need. I'm not a casual man, Lydia."

"I know."

He slowed the truck and turned onto his property. As they bounced along the rutted road, silence permeated the air much the way rotted fruit does.

He bounced to a stop, and Lydia was out of the truck before he had the key out of the ignition.

"Lydia—"

Lydia didn't turn around. Part of her wanted to. She couldn't explain it, but Evan felt like the other part of her soul. His love of his community, the land and the silence at the end of the day. These were the very things her hungry soul clamored for, but had never found.

The crunch of gravel under his boots warned her he was behind her before he touched her shoulder. His warmth burned through the thin layer of silk. She wished she were wearing a strapless evening gown so that he would touch her skin.

She took a deep breath, wanting to hide from him and the new emotions coursing through her. But her new life wasn't based on lies. Sure it isn't, she thought.

"I'm really not a casual woman. Though this isn't a place I'm familiar with, my flirting was not malicious."

Gently, he turned her until she faced him. His eyes were hidden behind aviator shades, and his face was hard. She wondered at her earlier fancy that this man was her soul mate.

"I know. But I want you too badly."

A tingle started at her shoulders and shot down her body, pooling at her center. "You want me?"

"Hell, yes! Don't tell me you don't know it."

"No man has ever wanted just me," she muttered to herself.

"I find that hard to believe."

"Oh, Evan," she said.

"Oh, what?"

He sounded frustrated and irritated. She couldn't help herself. Wrapping her arms around his neck, she kissed him.

His mouth was still under hers for a moment, and then he groaned and his arms came up, enfolding her. His big hand held her head, and his mouth plundered hers. She'd meant for their embrace to be a casual kiss—a kind of thank you—but Evan wasn't a casual man, especially when it came to kisses.

She was swept away in his embrace. His other hand roamed down her back, settling on the curves of her buttocks. His tongue thrust past the barrier of her teeth, and she opened her mouth to accept his intimate touch. She wanted more of him. Her heart pounded, and her body tingled. Her breasts ached for his touch, and her center felt empty.

She wanted his kiss to go on forever. She wanted him to carry her in the house to his bed upstairs, remove their clothing and make love to her in the primitive light of twilight.

Scared by the intensity of her reaction, she pulled back. His eyes were narrowed and his body hard. His breath rasped in and out, as hers did. As if they'd both run a marathon.

The warm exhalation of his air brushed over her

mouth and she wanted to have his lips on hers again. As his mouth descended, her body rejoiced, but her mind called out a warning. She knew that he was a man who could change her forever. She felt reborn into an oddly vulnerable creature.

A baby's cry came sharp and clear, startling them away from each other. Part of Lydia felt as if she'd received a reprieve, the other deeper part felt as if she'd missed something wonderful, and she regretted its loss.

Four

"Come and see what we have here," Evan said as he lifted a pink baby carrier from the porch swing. His voice was soft and soothing. An amazing thing in a man so big, Lydia thought.

She approached the man and baby with trepidation. She knew nothing about children, had never been close to one since childhood…except for her best friend Pam's son who'd thrown up on her new Vera Wang dress at his christening last summer.

The infant's cries increased to a frantic level. Poor thing, she thought. So scared and alone. Lydia would be the first to admit that her only maternal instinct was marveling over the tiny clothes made by Baby Dior, but she was moved by this little person, like her, alone in the world.

Peering around Evan she looked at the small being, crying for all it was worth, and felt her heart melt. No tears fell from the baby's tightly closed eyes, and its little body struggled to communicate its rage. Wrapped in a clean but worn blanket, this child was so different from her. Lydia took a moment to thank God for the fact that her father had always been able to make money out of nothing.

She reached out to touch the soft cheek, and the baby's head turned toward her finger. The baby suckled her finger. The baby's touch should have made her pull away, but it didn't. Instead she found herself, for the first time in her life, making a huge difference in someone's life. Wow.

Evan nudged her chin up, and she saw some indefinable emotion flash in his eyes. He reached out and brushed her cheek with his free hand. Shivers of awareness cascaded through her body.

His hand was rough and masculine, making her feel very womanly and feminine. The touch rekindled desires that were still smoldering. Evan freed the baby from the carrier and a piece of paper fluttered to the ground.

"Hold Jasmine for me."

Though she'd enjoyed the contact with the child, Lydia had no idea how to hold her. She put both hands around the child's middle and held her up. "How do you know her name?"

"It's pinned to her blanket."

"Oh."

"What are you doing?"

"Holding the baby."

"Cradle her in your arms."

"How?"

He stared at her for a minute, then adjusted the child until she lay against Lydia's chest. His fingers brushed the curve of her breast, and his hand under the baby's head was trapped for a minute. She looked into his gray gaze that wasn't icy now. There was a fire that burned away the superficial excesses of everyday life and saw straight to her core.

Evan's breath brushed against her cheek, and she wanted to lean that half-inch closer to him and touch her lips against his. She wanted to feel him strong with passion and reacting to her on the male-female level instead of keeping her at a distance and protecting himself.

The dogs barked and he stepped away. She felt bereft of his touch and alone again as he stooped to retrieve the note. The baby's tiny head nestled closer to Lydia's chest as she awkwardly rocked Jasmine back and forth.

"What does it say?" she asked. Her voice sounded soft and husky to her own ears.

"That her mother isn't ready to be a mom and her dad is out of the picture."

Lydia thanked goodness for her parents who, despite circumstances, had been strong together and always there for her. "How sad."

"It happens a lot."

Not in my world. ''What are we going to do with her?''

''We?''

''Well, I kind of like her even though I didn't know how to hold her.'' The baby was contentedly sucking away on Lydia's finger again.

''You're sure?''

''Yes. She's so sweet.'' She smelled like innocence. Baby powder and cuddly warm baby.

''She only seems that way now. Wait until you're diapering her.''

Lydia realized there was an entire world of baby functions she knew nothing about. The baby would be dependent on them for her every need until the authorities arrived to take her to her new home.

''What's the matter?'' Evan asked into the lengthening silence.

''I didn't realize how little I know about babies.''

''That's okay. You're not the type of woman who would know about babies.''

That remark resembled some of the things her fiancé had said to her. About being a socialite with more money than brains or common sense. Leaving the ditz behind, she'd tried to show Evan as much honesty as she could. In fact, he was the first man she'd ever laughed with in a genuine way.

''What kind of woman am I?'' she asked carefully. But she already knew the answer. Had heard from her father, who'd said pretty girls didn't need to know how to cook or clean.

''You remind me of my ex-wife, ready for a party and a night on the town. Not the kind of lady who's looking for a family.''

Though there was truth to his words, she hated to be judged and found wanting without evidence, because deep in her heart she did want a family. She'd never really had the opportunity to be around children. Her friends all had nannies who took care of their offspring while they skied in Vail or shopped in Paris. ''I'm not your ex-wife.''

''Amen.''

Not knowing what else to say, Lydia turned away and walked into the house with the baby. She stood in the dimly lit hallway holding baby Jasmine close to her chest. There was an undemanding acceptance in the baby's embrace that made her feel as if for once in her life who she was was good enough. As if Jasmine needed something only Lydia could give. As if life had finally shown her the place she was meant to be.

And Evan thought she wouldn't be able to handle this role. This roller-coaster day couldn't have any more ups and downs, she thought. She'd wanted to experience real life, but she'd had no idea it could hurt so much.

Evan watched her go and cursed himself. Her bright blue eyes had dimmed a little when he'd said she was a party girl. Twilight darkened into evening, and he watched the last of the sun's rays dip beyond the horizon. For a day that had been okay, it had gone downhill quickly. He'd had no business kissing her.

Yet the temptation had been too much. He still wanted her. The one way he and a city woman always got along was in the bedroom. Lydia flirted like a world champion, yet she kissed like an innocent. Like it was the first time she'd felt a man's passion and an equal one of her own.

He'd have seduced her outside with all the finesse of a high school boy in the backseat of his daddy's car with his first girlfriend. But she deserved better. But he'd always been a coarse man. The kind who should never be left alone with a delicate lady.

He was the perfect man when you were backed against the wall in a life-or-death situation, but the softer emotions—hell they weren't for him. Shanna had taught him that. And she'd been right.

And whoever Lydia really was she was most definitely a delicate lady. She had a grace and sophistication that Placid Springs had never seen. He'd lashed out to remind himself that despite the perfection of the picture of woman and child, she wasn't really suited to the role. She'd light out of town faster than a tourist during a hurricane once she realized how much time a baby involved.

Hefting the pink-and-white diaper bag and the car seat in one hand, Evan paused to examine his own home, afraid to enter. Hell, some tough hombre he was.

An angry one-hundred-twenty-pound blonde was

enough to stop him. He realized suddenly that it wasn't Lydia keeping him from entering the house but his own instincts. The last time his pulse had raced this heavily he'd ended up heartbroken and alone.

The baby's cries drifted out the open window, and he heard Lydia's low voice soothing the child. But baby Jasmine wasn't content with the lullaby. Evan knew enough about babies to know that if rocking and singing wasn't getting the job done then it was time for diapering or feeding.

He walked into the house expecting the cold shoulder. He'd hurt her feelings and now he'd have to pay for it with a week or two of the sulks. Maybe she'd be gone by then, he thought.

Maybe he could keep his pants zipped and his hands to himself. If he looked into those deep blue eyes of hers again and saw her watching him with feminine interest, he wasn't going to be able to walk away.

He nearly collided with Lydia as she hurried back down the hallway. Dropping the car seat and bag, he wrapped a steadying arm around Lydia and the baby.

"Evan, thank God. I don't know what's wrong with her. She just keeps crying."

She needed him. He was tempted to believe what his eyes were telling his mind, but his heart knew better. This sweet concerned woman was really the sophisticated sexy lady who'd kissed his socks off outside.

He let her go and stepped back, retreating to safety in a gruff manner that would make her keep her distance. "Let's go in the kitchen and see what we can do about Jasmine."

He snagged the baby's stuff and led the way down the hall. The kitchen was dimly lit and intimate, he realized when Lydia entered the room right behind him.

She'd shifted Jasmine to her shoulder and was rocking her back and forth. "I don't think this is working."

"Take it easy," he said, brushing his hand over the baby's head. He rummaged through the diaper bag, pulling out a diaper and a can of dry baby formula.

"You were right. I'm not mother material."

The sadness in her voice made him want to be wrong. But when it came to kids and parents he seldom was. He had a sixth sense about the ability of a man or woman to parent their own child, and he'd never been wrong. In fact, the FBI had used him in their special crimes division before he'd returned to Placid Springs.

"I think she might be hungry or wet. You want to heat the bottle or change her?" he asked, ignoring her comment.

Lydia looked skeptical. "You can do those things?"

"Sure." He wasn't that good at it. Truth to tell as much as he loved babies, they were so tiny he felt too big around them. But he'd always been able to get any job done.

"I'd rather heat the bottle," he said.

"Okay. I watched my best friend diaper her son at his christening. So I should be able to do this."

She took the diaper and a package of baby wipes and set them aside. It only took her five tries to get the diaper properly on the baby. Evan watched her in the reflection cast on the window as he heated the bottle and tried not let the scene affect him. But his heart felt a ray of hope. Here was the woman he'd always searched for. And she wasn't for him.

The porch swing creaked as Lydia put it in motion. She'd always imagined the country to be quiet, but the cattle and night bugs were creating a symphony for her. It was chilly, and she wrapped her arms around her body while she looked up at the stars.

Baby Jasmine was now carefully tucked away in the cradle that Payne had built for Evan. Lydia had never seen two bachelors handle a baby with the ease and expertise of Evan and his father. She was in awe of them.

Evan was on the phone with Child Services trying to find a home for Jasmine. Lydia was oddly relieved to know the baby would be leaving soon. As connected as she felt to the tiny infant, the baby also made her feel inadequate. What kind of woman didn't know about babies?

The kind who'd never been around them, she thought. She'd wanted a family once upon a long ago. Men always flocked around her because of her looks and money, and she'd never had to sit home a single

Friday night. But she didn't trust those men with their smooth airs and suave looks. She didn't like the way they looked at her as if she were nothing more than an ornament.

She wanted to be taken for substance not for fluff, but life hadn't ever offered her the chance to prove her worth until now. She sat a little straighter and thought again of baby Jasmine. She could handle the baby—even though Evan thought she was nothing more than a pretty face. What had he called her—a city woman?

She was smart. She'd figure out how to handle the baby and master those skills better than any country woman.

The screen door creaked, and Evan stepped onto the porch. Back-lit by the hall light he looked gruff and a little menacing. She shivered and leaned against the back of the swing.

"What are you doing out here?" he asked, his voice a raspy whisper that brought goose bumps to her skin.

"Thinking."

"Of…?"

You, she thought. Because at the moment all she could remember was the feel of his mouth against hers. She wanted to be in his arms, pressing her aching breasts to his chest and letting passion rule for once.

He walked forward. Lydia fancied that he'd read her mind and was coming to kiss her. Coming to her to take her to the plane they'd been on before the baby's cry had brought them back to reality. It wasn't a plane that owed anything to her reluctance to tell him her true identity but a plane of two adults who couldn't wait another moment to be in each other's arms.

He canted one hip against the porch railing and leaned against a support post. Her silly heart beat a bit faster as she watched him. Dammit, she had to learn to control her physical response to him.

"Lydia?"

She blinked and focused on Evan as he stood before her. Evan Powell wasn't the type of man who'd let passion dominate his life. Despite the depth of their embrace, she'd sensed he was holding part of himself back.

She glanced out into the deepening night. The voices of the ranch hands drifted up from the bunkhouse.

"I was thinking about the baby. When will Child Services be here?"

"They're not coming. I'm going to have to keep the baby for a few days while I run a check for her parents. My dad and I are approved foster parents with the county system so it's not unusual for this to happen. Dad will stay at home instead of going out with the men."

"Can I help?"

"How?"

"I could stay here and keep her during the day instead of working in your office."

"You didn't even know how to hold the baby earlier."

Lydia sat up straighter. "I diapered her and fed her."

"Yes, you did."

"Well. It's not as if you have a lot of choices, and I do owe you something for letting me stay here."

"You don't owe me a thing. I'll pay you the same as I would have if you'd come to the office."

"Only if you feel you must," she said, thinking of the experience she'd gain. Looking forward to learning more about the baby and mothering, Lydia felt a sense of purpose she hadn't known she was searching for.

"I do."

Silence settled between them. The comfortable kind that she imagined fell between happily married husbands and wives. In fact it was too comfortable. Her life was in flux, she needed to remember that the sheriff wasn't a man she could afford to fall in love with. And that was a real danger because she liked him.

Liked the way he cared about his small town and his dad. Liked the way he knew what to do about babies but didn't feel comfortable doing it. Liked the way he kissed her as if he was parched and she was the only woman on the earth who could quench his thirst.

She stared at him for a moment and found his eyes on her. A slow heavy heat moved through her body, sweeping from her neck slowly down her breasts and pooling in her center. Go to him, her impulses screamed.

"I'm going to—good night."

Standing, she walked quickly toward the screen door. He caught her arm when she would have passed him.

"Don't I get a good-night kiss?" he asked. His deep voice had dropped another level, and he pulled her body against his. He was lean and hard, and his legs, encased in denim, felt rough against the silk of her skirt.

She gazed up at him. His eyes appeared blacker than midnight in the dim light.

His hands settled on her hips as he drew her closer. She could feel his hardness brush against the notch between her legs. She melted against him, wanting a more direct touch, needing more than he was offering, knowing this was all she might have.

"Oh."

"Yes, oh."

Leaning up, she brushed a kiss against his cheek and stepped back. She wanted to linger, but not right now. She was still raw from the way he'd looked at her holding the baby and told her she wasn't the maternal type. Still raw from the passion he'd evoked in her earlier. Still aching from the realization that life had finally offered her the one thing she craved.

"Goodnight, Evan."

She walked into the house and the screen door cracked closed behind her.

"Lydia?"

"Yes."

"I'm going to want answers in the morning about your past."

"Okay," she said, walking away. Funny how the problems she'd left behind didn't seem as big any more. She was far more worried about the baby and Evan than her father and her purchased fiancé.

Five

Evan and his dad returned from the morning chores to find Lydia covered in baby cereal and the baby nowhere in sight. Evan bit the inside of his lip to keep from smiling at the icy-blonde who now bore little resemblance to the elegant woman who'd first arrived on his doorstep. Her guard was down, and she was the tiniest bit vulnerable. Her patrician features were covered in drying baby food.

"You look good enough to eat, sugar."

"One more word, Powell..." Lydia said, waving a finger at him.

His dad laughed. "I believe I'll eat with the boys in the mess hall this morning."

Payne exited without another word. Evan watched

his dad go, feeling lighter than he had in years. Something about the sassy way that Lydia moved through life made his soul lighter.

"I'm sorry, I didn't mean that the way it sounded. I'm having a tough morning."

"I wasn't offended."

"Scared?" she taunted. Her gaze skimmed down his body, and he hardened in a rush. More than anything he longed to have her back in his arms as he had had last night, and this time he wasn't going to let her just walk away.

"Nope, but if you want to kiss me I won't object."

"I'll bet."

He wanted her. Especially looking the way she did at this moment. A close glance revealed she was wearing one of his dress shirts tied at the waist and a pair of snug designer jeans.

"Is that my shirt?"

"I hope you don't mind. It was chilly this morning, and I only packed short-sleeved blouses."

He suspected she didn't want to soil her expensive clothing, but he didn't mind her wearing his shirt. In fact, he'd like to see her wearing nothing but his shirt.

"Where's Jasmine?"

"Napping. She fell asleep while she was drinking her bottle."

"You sure you want to take care of her?"

"Yes. Despite the way this looks, we had a successful feeding."

Evan fixed himself a bowl of cold cereal. "Good. Are you ready to tell me what you're hiding from?"

Her body said no, but she nodded. He leaned against the Spanish-tiled counter and ate his breakfast.

"Are you running from a husband?" he asked. It was that worry that concerned him most. He'd kissed and flirted with her. If she stayed in his house for the two weeks it would take to repair her car, he'd probably sleep with her.

"No."

He swallowed another spoonful of cereal. "What then?"

"My family."

He waited. A long time ago he'd figured out that men and women hated silence and would do anything to fill it. Patience had served him well in the FBI crime lab, and it would work now.

"My dad is on this kick for me to marry one of his executives, and I'm not ready. I thought I was, but..."

She bit her lower lip and stared at the hardwood floor as if it held the answer to a deep mystery. "What, sugar?"

"I want more than an arranged marriage."

"Don't you have a boyfriend back home?"

"No. I don't date much."

"I figured a woman like you would have men six deep around her, calling to ask her out."

She shrugged. "Sometimes."

"So what's the problem? Tell your dad you want more from marriage than what he's proposed."

"I can't. He's obsessed with finding me a husband."

"Then pick one."

"I did—one of my dad's VP's."

"So you *are* married."

"No. I was engaged. But my fiancé didn't want the same things from marriage that I did."

He didn't need any more answers from her. She'd given him enough information to settle his mind on the question of who she was, but he needed more. He wanted to strip away the civilized layers of sophistication and find the woman beneath the lady. The woman who volunteered to care for a foundling even though appearances clearly announced that she was from the upper class and could easily pay for a nanny.

"What do you want?"

"Passion, lust, monogamy, love."

"In that order?" he asked, because he knew women seldom put love last, and a woman like Lydia deserved love first.

"No. I want to marry for love."

He knew it. Hell, she deserved love second and third too. She was the type of woman who needed a good, strong man who could flirt with her and cuddle with her. Not a burnt-out small-town sheriff who couldn't love.

Even his dad, whom he cared deeply about, wasn't a demonstrative man. He assumed his dad would miss him if he died, but words had never been exchanged between them. Even when a heart attack had laid the old man up in the hospital and they'd been afraid Payne would die, neither had been able to say the words. Sometimes he thought that might be why Shanna had left him.

"Why can't you marry for love?"

"Because I was raised to be an ornament."

Those words obviously weren't her own. "You're not an ornament."

"I know, but men don't seem to."

"I noticed," he said.

"But you're not looking for love."

He couldn't answer her. Could only watch as she turned and walked away. Damn, he was getting tired of watching her leave, but she'd made a point. He couldn't offer her love, and she'd confirmed that it was the one thing she needed.

A couple of nights later, Lydia still felt raw from her encounter with Evan. She'd avoided him, needing to prove to herself that she could handle Jasmine on her own, and knowing she'd be tempted to let him carry her burdens on his broad shoulders.

And this time you're making it on your own, she reminded herself.

Florida was a surprisingly nice place to live. Or she should say Placid Springs was. She'd visited the one grocery store in town. A mom-and-pop place that still ran a credit list at the register. She'd learned that Evan had been a straight-A student in high school but had tended to be a troublemaker. Evan was so much a part of the town that she couldn't imagine one without the other.

She'd wanted to tease him about it, but knew she needed to put distance between them. And from the beginning his sense of humor and teasing smile had been more than she could resist.

She wanted to know more about the complex man who was becoming less than a stranger to her. He'd already moved beyond that, she acknowledged.

At this point in her life she didn't need a man complicating things. And although what Evan wanted was direct and uncomplicated, she needed more and wasn't about to give her heart away again.

Lydia slid into bed and shut off the light. The sheets smelled like sunlight. She closed her eyes, imagining herself in the sun. There was a simplicity to this way of life she'd never imagined. There was no rushing to make a lunch appointment, no finessing of a difficult businessman who didn't want to cough up the money she needed to successfully launch an event. Nothing but Jasmine and her needs.

She stared at the patterns of the moon and clouds on the ceiling. The window was open, and a cool breeze blew through her room. She'd never slept with the windows open before. It was soothing. The sounds outside and the security of knowing Evan was down the hall if she needed help during the night should have eased her way to dreamland.

But Evan was the very reason she couldn't sleep, knowing she'd dream again of him and his hot hands on her body. She'd woken last night with the sheets in a tangle and her body throbbing.

How she wanted him. She'd always thought lust something that only shallow people engaged in. But experiencing it now, she understood the power of attraction in a wholly new way.

It made her engagement seem so superficial. Already she'd experienced more with Evan than she ever had with Paul. Poor, Paul. It was a good thing he'd had the sense to find another woman, because Lydia realized now that she could never have loved him.

Jasmine's cry brought her from the bed in one bound. She headed across the hall for the temporary nursery. The nightlight illuminated the crib.

A big part of her was still scared she'd hurt the baby, or do something to endanger its safety with her ignorance of mothering. Yet another part of her said that this was what she was meant to do.

She picked Jasmine up, holding her close, and the baby's cries stopped for a minute, her small body trembling in the aftermath of all those tears.

Rubbing her hand down the baby's back, Lydia realized that Jasmine was beginning to recognize her. The baby couldn't be more than nine months old, but she was increasingly secure around Lydia.

Changing Jasmine's diaper and then refastening her sleeper, she placed the baby back in the crib, wrapping her snugly in the pink blanket they'd found her in. She positioned a little stuffed lamb that she'd purchased in town two days ago, and watched the baby find a comfortable position and then fall asleep.

"Everything okay in here?" Evan asked from the door. His voice rasped softly in the intimately lit room.

"Yes."

A quick glance showed the baby was sleeping again and Lydia followed Evan out of the room.

"Join me for a cup of cocoa?"

She knew she shouldn't, but she'd missed his sharp wit and keen intelligence. For the last two days she'd engaged in baby talk with a nine-month-old baby. She was hungry for adult conversation.

"Let me grab my robe."

"Don't get it on my account," he said, his gaze sweeping over her.

The negligee she wore was revealing. Did he find her sexy and tempting in it? Her nipples hardened, and her breath became shorter.

He was wearing only a pair of tight, faded jeans, and she'd give a few years off her life to caress his chest. His muscles weren't over-developed but were sculpted from years of hard work on the ranch.

He stepped closer, still leaving a respectable six inches between them. She closed her eyes and breathed in the scent of man. Raw and masculine, strong and powerful.

She scooted closer—half an inch—peeking at him through half-closed eyes. His own visage was harsh now as arousal changed him.

She lifted her hand, saw the difference in her pale

skin next to the bronzed elegance of his. Her fingers brushed gently against his shoulder and then across his chest. Her touch followed the line of chest hair that disappeared into the waistband of his denims.

His breath rasped between his teeth, and she glanced up at him. He was watching her carefully. His body still and hard.

His hand swept down the front of her body, caressing her shoulders and neck. His palm was callused and should have been rough but was instead exciting. He fondled her nipples through thin barrier of her silk nightgown.

She swayed closer to him, needing more of his touch. He groaned and pulled her closer. His hand locking in her hair as his mouth took hers in a kiss that was frankly carnal.

Even though she wanted to let nature take its course, she knew she'd be leading him on. She cared for Evan in a way she'd never cared for any man before, and she didn't want to hurt him.

She stepped back. "Wow."

He just looked at her. Honesty demanded she say something to him. Tell him exactly what was going on inside her head. No matter what the cost to herself.

"I'm sorry, but I want more than lust from you."

He nodded. "I suspected as much."

"I think I'll skip the cocoa."

She pivoted and walked slowly toward her room because she wanted to run. She felt his gaze on her as she walked and it made each step awkward. She felt the sway of fabric against her legs as her hips swayed.

"Lydia."

"Yes," she said, glancing over her shoulder.

"Sooner or later it's not going to matter any more, you know that don't you?"

She forced herself to finish walking to her bedroom door and leaned against the doorframe.

"Aren't you going to answer?"

"Did you want one?"

"You know I did."

"You're right. I'm just hoping both of us are prepared to handle the consequences."

"I am."

"Don't be so sure, Sheriff. You're not the tough guy you think you are," she said, and firmly closed the door.

"Duchess is feeling high and mighty this morning," Payne said, when Evan entered the stall. "Watch her hindquarters."

"Dad, I've been working with horses all my life. I think I know what to do." It was his day off from the sheriff's office, and they were mending a fence. Normally he enjoyed his days at home, but Lydia had him in a constant state of arousal. Even his Tae Kwon Do workout wasn't enough to focus his mind and body.

"I know. You seem distracted lately."

Evan knew his father was right but ignored him. He had enough on his plate without adding a meddlesome father. Part of the reason they got along so well was a healthy respect for each other's space.

"I ever tell you about the time I got gored by a steer while I was courting your mom?"

Oh, no. "Yes."

"Enough said."

Evan led the mare out of the stall and began to saddle her. His father thought all Evan needed was the love of a good woman to make his life complete. Evan knew better. This small community, his charming hometown, was an anachronism to the outside world.

Tourists liked to stop and eat at the fifties-style diner in the middle of town and have their pictures taken beside the imitation gas lamps that lined Main Street. But no one wanted to live this far from real civilization.

They didn't have a local Internet provider, cable television or a take-out Chinese restaurant. But Evan wouldn't have it any other way. He liked knowing that if he walked into the barbershop on Tuesday, Gus would be getting a trim. He liked that everyone in town knew his history and that he knew theirs.

But women, especially city women, needed something different. And Lydia Martin, if that really was her name, certainly wanted more than this small town and its sheriff had to give.

His father led Porter, a gelding, out and began to saddle him. He had a sudden image of himself at sixty-five doing the same thing. Living the same cold, lonely existence, and it was sobering. Maybe it was time to settle down again. Find a woman who'd lived in Placid Springs all her life and understood the nuances of small-town living.

Maybe a Sunday-school teacher, except that they were all his dad's age and remembered him from his "wild" childhood. Ah, hell. The only woman in town that he was interested in would be leaving in a couple of weeks.

"Dad, she's not like mom."

Payne grunted but didn't say anything. Even though it was the same technique Evan had used on Lydia the day before, Payne's silence worked on him now.

"She's from a big city. You can see that she doesn't belong here."

"All I see is you pushing her away."

His dad could be a nosey old coot. But, as usual, he was right on the money. "That's right, I am. Leave it be."

"I want some grandkids before I die. I know I ain't got much longer to live. You know it too."

Evan shook his head. The old man would probably outlive him. "You'll be around for your grandkids."

"That mean you're planning to remarry?"

"Someday. To a nice local girl who's happy living right here."

"Not every woman is Shanna." His dad was shrewd about human nature and had warned him not to marry young, but Evan had always wanted a big family and had wanted to start on his own early. Now, when he thought of a wife and children, all he saw was a certain icy-blonde who was giving him the cold shoulder.

But there was something about Lydia that called to his soul. Something about the sadness in her eyes and the loneliness he sensed in her soul that made him want to take a chance on a woman again.

"I know," he said to his dad.

"That little gal you got watching the baby is stronger than she looks." Payne swung onto his horse like a man who'd done it every day of his life.

"How do you figure?" Evan asked, mounting his own horse.

"She's cooked your goose a time or two. I've never seen any woman stand up to you the way she does."

"Evan?" Lydia called before entering the barn, saving him from a reply he didn't want to make.

"Yes?"

With the baby propped on her hip, she looked like a real mom, not a woman pinch-hitting for a few days. She wore a polo shirt with the collar raised in the back and a slim straight khaki skirt that ended above her knees. She had great legs. He wished he'd slid his hand under her nightgown the other night.

"What time will you be back for lunch?"

"About noon, why?"

"Jasmine is usually napping then. Please be quiet when you come in."

"Thanks for telling us, Lydia. You're going to make some baby a fine mother," Payne said.

Lydia blushed. "I'm not really that good at it."

"You'll do, girl," Payne said, riding out.

Evan watched her shift the baby from one hip to the other. Jasmine was holding on to a stuffed animal of some kind, and Lydia juggled baby and toy with an ease she hadn't had a few days ago.

"Your dad is quite a flatterer."

"Not really." In fact Payne rarely had much to say about anyone, but he did seem to like Lydia. He'd have to warn the old man not to get too close to her. She wasn't staying.

"Well. Have a good day," she said, and turned to walk away.

But he sensed her sadness and cursed himself for the coarse man he was. He'd been raised around ranch hands. His mother had tried, God rest her soul, but her influence wasn't enough to contradict what he saw day-in and day-out.

"The town is celebrating its Heritage Day tomorrow. Will you and Jasmine join me for a picnic in the park?"

She nodded and walked away. He knew she'd been waiting to hear him say something nice about her mothering. And she was doing a great job. But he didn't want to acknowledge that she might be more than a flirty sexy blonde. If he did, he didn't know how he'd keep her at bay.

Six

The lakeshore was dotted with families and blankets. Skiers and fisherman vied for prime locations on the water. Music drifted through the air with the same laziness as the breeze, and, though it was hot, Lydia felt comfortable in a way she never had before.

Lying back on the blanket, with the baby playing next to her, she felt a sense of rightness that had been missing from her life for a long, long time. The Heritage Day celebration was an event the citizens of Placid Springs took very seriously. She'd heard tales about the open range and how it had lasted until the 1940s. And how tourism was ruining the state.

Lydia had never been to a Heritage Day celebration, but she'd envisioned a big-name live band and maybe some first-class catered food. Instead, a group of old-timers played bluegrass on banjos and six-strings. The food was prepared in a big barbecue pit, and all the men in town took turns cooking. And it exceeded her imagination. Evan's shift was over, and she hoped he'd join them soon.

Lydia was aware of the looks she and Jasmine received, and she'd heard more than one man giving Evan a hard time about his "found-family." But for the most part it was good-natured. She hugged the baby closer thankful to have someone else with her who didn't fit into this warm community.

Evan joined them with plates piled high with food. "Hungry?"

Starving, actually, but for more than food. Since she'd left him in the hallway the other night she'd been unable to sleep.

"This is a great town," Lydia said, once Evan was seated and they each had a plate of food.

"Yeah, it is."

An elderly couple waved to Evan, and he paused to return the gesture and call out a greeting. The brief conversation ended quickly, but made Lydia realize how much a part of this town Evan was. He'd never be happy anywhere else, she thought.

"Where's your dad today?" she asked, when the couple had moved on.

He chuckled. "With the widow Jenkins, but I'm not supposed to know."

"Why? Were you close to your mom?"

He took his time chewing and swallowing before answering. "I was. He thinks he's protecting me."

Lydia understood more than Evan probably thought she did. "My dad is the same way."

The baby cooed a little but was content to lie on her back and stare up at the changing patterns of shadow and sun revealed in the tree's leaves.

"Any word on your car?"

"Yes. The mechanic said it will take seven to ten more days for the part he needs to be delivered. Then I'll be out of your hair."

He looked out over the lake. "You're not in my hair."

Those few words quieted the restless place inside her. And though common sense dictated that he was just being nice, she was touched. "I'm not really very domestic."

"I noticed."

She smiled at him. "It'd be hard not to."

"Yeah, that burnt smell seems to linger in the kitchen."

Well, at least he was talking about her cooking and not the drapery she'd caught in the vacuum. "Cooking is harder than it looks."

"You're welcome to eat with the hands down at the bunkhouse."

"I'm not much on mingling," she said. She'd always hated that part of parties, preferring instead to plan and execute them, to stand in the kitchen and direct staff. For a minute she wished she were back in her father's mansion with nothing more to worry about than what wine went with what course.

"Me either," he said, quietly.

But he charmed everyone he met so he wouldn't have to mingle at a party. He'd be the type who people would try to get close to.

"It must help that everyone in town knows you."

"Yeah. That's kind of weird though."

"I think it's charming."

"Of course you do."

"What's that mean?"

"Just that you seem lonely."

How had he seen past the shell she used to protect herself? "Lonely? No way. I'm very active at home. It's just that I don't know many people here, and there isn't a way for me to meet them."

"Does your soul know that, Lydia?" he asked. The quietly spoken words cut straight to her heart like a warm knife through butter.

She glanced away from him and the honesty of the moment. There had been something missing from her life for a long time. She'd thought about it long and hard and knew it had started when her mother had died. But she'd never been able to identify anything that would fill the gap in her life.

"No."

He brushed his hand across her hair, and she wanted to lean closer to him. She wanted to rest her head on his big, strong chest but didn't, because she didn't want to lead him on. The other night had shown her she had no will power where this man was concerned.

"I don't know how to connect with these people."

"Make small talk. Practice on me."

She set her plate aside and focused on her stock questions, the ones she used to survive at her father's parties.

"Where did you vacation this winter? Did you ski Vail?"

"Not a good question to start with unless you want to do all the talking. No one here has been out of the town this winter."

"What should I say?"

"What do you do? Tell me about your family."

"Tell me about your family," she said.

His eyes had locked onto hers, and she felt that he was boring his way straight to her soul, examining every inch of her that was revealed. She felt around for her sunglasses and found the baby chewing on them. Damn. She wanted the protection they would offer but didn't want to deprive the baby of her toy.

"It's just my dad and me."

She leaned a little closer, watching his firm, hard mouth as he formed his answers. "No brothers or sisters?"

"Nope. Always wanted a big family, but my mom had medical problems."

"Oh, me too."

"Wanted a bigger family?"

"Yes. It was hard living up to the demands put on

me by my parents. It would have been nice to share that with someone. I really wanted a sister.''

But she'd always been close to her dad. In fact, she'd called his secretary yesterday morning and left a message that she was okay and would be in touch later.

''Me too. Someone I could look after.''

''Instead you're looking after the entire town.''

He nodded. One of his deputies stepped over, and Evan stood to talk to him.

Lydia found Jasmine another toy and cleaned her designer frames before slipping them on. She needed to keep the sheriff at a distance, not let him get closer, even though the thought of having him closer made her heart beat faster.

They began to gather up the picnic stuff after the deputy moved on. Lydia settled the baby in her carrier and started to stand. Evan offered her a hand, and she took it. His palm was warm and callused, and she never wanted to let it go. But she had to, because she could never survive in a small town and Evan Powell couldn't survive outside of one.

Evan watched Lydia as she moved inside the house. The light played over her skin like an attentive lover. She fascinated him. She tempted him the way forbidden fruit had tempted man since the beginning of time.

He wished he were a stronger man. He wished she were a different woman, the kind who'd be content to live in a small town. He wished he were able to turn away but couldn't.

His dogs rushed around the corner, barking and making more noise than the law allowed. He greeted them and stomped up the stairs, having no choice but to make his presence known. He'd avoided her since they'd arrived home from the Heritage Day celebration by spending unnecessary time in the barn grooming his favorite horse.

The fireworks had scared the baby, and Lydia had comforted her in a way that he'd never expected his pampered princess to. A bond had been formed between Lydia and the baby that he didn't understand, but that enchanted him. She'd changed, from the woman who hadn't known how to hold a child. She'd changed and he knew he owed her an apology for the comparison he'd made between her and his ex-wife.

Watching Lydia and the baby had created a longing in him he'd never expected to experience. He wanted her. But more than that, he wanted to mate with her and make her the mother of his children. It didn't matter that his conscious mind said she wasn't the right woman to mother his children. His body and soul cried out that she was.

"Evan?"

He knew he shouldn't answer, that his control was tenuous at the moment and it would take little provocation on her part to push him over the edge. "Yes?"

"Are you coming in?"

"No."

She came to the screen door, silhouetted by the light in the hall. Her sundress was clingy, and all day long he'd tortured himself with thoughts of what she had on underneath. Now he knew. Nothing. She was bare. The night breeze tightened her nipples. He wanted to taste her. To see if she'd taste as sweet as he imagined she would.

His manhood strained the inseam of his jeans and he adjusted himself discreetly. But comfort couldn't be found. The only thing that could relieve him was Lydia.

"I enjoyed the picnic today. Can you believe that's the first one I've ever been to?" Lydia stepped out of the house onto the porch. He noticed she'd touched up her lipstick, a deep pink color that drew his eye.

Evan backed down the steps to the ground, keeping distance between them. "Shouldn't you be upstairs with the baby?"

"I put the monitor on the hall table, so we could hear her. It's such a lovely night, I want to enjoy it."

"It's just a summer evening."

"No, it's not. There's magic in the air, can't you feel it?"

No, he couldn't feel anything but the blood pulsing through his veins and the need pushing him back onto the porch. She sat on the swing and leaned her head back, letting her long hair fall loosely down her back. Her graceful neck was exposed, and all he could think about was kissing her there. Nipping gently with his teeth and working his way down to her breasts.

"Sit with me?" she asked.

He crossed to her, unable to talk. Taking his hand in hers she started the swing in motion. She licked her lips and he tracked the movement with his gaze, wishing he were the one brushing his tongue across her flesh.

"When I was a little girl I used to imagine fireflies were fairies. They'd circle around the pool and I'd try to catch them."

She was sweet, and he knew that her life was changing. He could see it in her eyes, but his life wasn't ever going to change. And he wanted to taste sweetness just once.

"Did you ever catch them?"

"No. Mother said ladies don't play with bugs."

He wondered at her childhood. How had she grown into the perfect princess she was today? But tonight she didn't seem like the aloof icy-blonde who'd arrived on his doorstep injured and in trouble. Tonight her guard was down, and her defenses would be easily breached.

"Evan…"

"Yes."

"Do you remember the other night when I was wearing my nightgown?"

Hell, yes. He grunted. He'd thought of little else during the day and her image had plagued his dreams.

"I wish we hadn't stopped."

She was killing him. He was hanging on by a

thread, and she was snipping at it with sharp scissors of desire.

"Do you?"

"Sugar, don't tease me tonight. I want you."

She opened those sleepy eyes of hers and stared right at him. "Good."

She leaned forward, her breasts brushing his upper arm. He held her away. He had to give her one last chance to choose while he could still stop.

"I'm still not offering you more than lust."

Her eyes darkened with sadness, but she didn't pull away. "That's okay."

"Then come here, sugar, because I've been good for too long, and I'm dying to have at least one lick."

He curved his arm around her shoulder, pulling her flush with his body. Her rounded curves fit nicely against the planes of his body, but all he could think of was those deep pink lips—full and pouty—and how he wanted to plunder their depths. He tipped her head back until it rested on his shoulder and lowered his mouth to hers.

Tracing the seam of her lips with his tongue as he'd fantasized earlier, he wanted to let the sensations she generated in him build. Instead passion overwhelmed him, and he couldn't wait. He had to taste the inside of her mouth. He had to know all of her feminine secrets. The secrets that she hid from him with a sweep of her long black eyelashes.

Her nails scraped along his leg, moving inexorably higher. His groin tightened even more.

He stopped her hand before it could move any higher, shifting her touch instead to his shoulder. He pulled her onto his lap, so he could explore her fully. Her mouth opened fully under his, and she moaned in the back of her throat. An answering primal cry came from deep within him.

He traced the hard outline of her nipple against the soft fabric of her silk dress. The twin sensation of silky softness and hardened flesh made him long for a bed. He wanted to see her draped across his big king-sized model, wearing nothing but sunlight. He needed to lie her back and taste her flesh. Her mouth was exquisite, doing things to him he'd forgotten, if he'd ever experienced them at all before.

He broke free of her mouth and nibbled his way down her neck. Her hands tightened in his hair, guiding him closer to her breasts.

"What do you want, sugar?"

"Don't you know?"

"I want you to tell me."

"Kiss me again."

"Here?" he asked, brushing his lips against hers.

"No."

"Here?" he asked, gently biting the curve of her neck.

"No."

"Where, sugar?"

She guided his head to her breast and lifted her body to him. "Here."

He moaned as his teeth closed over her tightened

nipple and he suckled strongly. He felt as if something deep inside himself was being nourished by Lydia. Being nourished by the sweetness inside her. Being nourished and given the seeds of growth, but he couldn't define it. Didn't want to define anything while this tempting woman filled his arms and his mouth.

Harsh voices sounded from the bunkhouse. Evan lifted his head from Lydia's breast, feeling much like a bull being ridden for the first time.

"What is that?" Lydia asked, her arms covering the damp circle on her chest.

"My men."

She still looked dazed. Her lips were red and swollen now. Her skin flushed with passion, and her breasts trembled under her crossed arms.

"Dammit, woman, I'm not ready to stop."

"Me either," she said.

"I have to see to them."

"I know. There will be another time," she said.

She stood and walked into the house, the door slamming shut behind her. Dammit, she'd walked away from him again. He didn't know why, but it bothered the hell out of him that she kept leaving.

Jasmine was fussier than usual the next day, but Lydia had a new confidence where the baby was concerned. Evan had praised her mothering skills that morning. True, he'd only said she was doing an okay job of taking care of the baby. But she knew how hard certain words were for him and took them as the praise she was sure he meant them to be.

She'd spent most of the day driving the baby up and down the rutted ranch road in a battered Jeep Evan had offered for her use until her car was fixed, which was the only way she could get Jasmine to stop crying. Lydia stared down at the small child she'd come to care for, and didn't know what to do next. She wouldn't eat, she couldn't sleep and her diaper was clean and dry.

Holding the baby carefully against her chest she rocked with her on the hardwood living-room floor. The clock read 8:00 p.m. Normally, Jasmine would be in bed and asleep by this time. Lydia realized she didn't know as much about mothering as she'd believed.

Maybe she *was* only meant to be an ornament. Maybe because of her genes she was the kind of mother who was supposed to have a nanny who did all the work. But that didn't feel right. Tears of frustration burned her eyes, and she stood and began pacing the room with the child.

The familiar sound of Evan's truck broke through Jasmine's cries, and Lydia headed for the front door. Evan ran toward them as they stepped out of the house. The concern on his face touched her deep in the recesses of her hidden heart.

"What's wrong, sugar?"

Lydia tried to speak but couldn't control her crying.

She took a deep breath of air. ''I'm not good with children.''

''Sure you are.''

''No I'm not. I've tried everything, Evan. And she's still crying. I think I may have done something wrong.''

''You didn't.''

''How do you know that? You were the one who said I was not the kind of lady who's looking for a family.''

Evan paled and ushered her and the baby into the house. ''Take Jasmine in the living room while I call the doctor.''

''His service is paging him,'' Lydia said.

''Which doctor did you call?''

''Dr. Green. He's the only one listed in the book.''

He looked uncomfortable. Probably afraid for the baby. Jasmine continued to cry, her whole body tensing. Lydia bent and brushed a small kiss to the baby's forehead.

''Doesn't anything help?''

''Riding around in the truck.''

''Why don't I take her for a ride while you wait for the doctor's call?''

''It doesn't last. As soon as you get out of the car, she starts crying again.''

He reached for her. And Lydia wanted to go to him. To put her head on his big shoulders and let him carry this burden for her, but she knew that was the weak way out. She'd determined to be a strong woman after her car accident.

And she had been. True, she wasn't overly maternal, but she'd been a good caregiver for the baby before this. She wasn't domestic, but she'd tried, darn it. And she'd let Evan get close to her. Closer than he'd probably wanted to be emotionally but not nearly close enough physically.

She knew then that she had to leave. That the only solution to this mess was to take herself out of the picture.

"I'm sorry," she said, thrusting the baby toward him.

He didn't take her; only stared at Lydia with unreadable eyes, his dark gaze, which she'd seen alive with passion and humor and sometimes frustration, closed to her.

"Don't be so hard on yourself."

"I'm not being any harder on myself than you've been."

She placed the baby against his chest, and he hugged Jasmine close. Lydia felt an intense longing to be held that way but didn't give in to it. Instead she dropped another kiss on the baby's cheek and glanced around the room where she'd spent so much time playing with Jasmine.

Through the open window she could see the porch swing in the deepening twilight. The place where she'd almost made love with Evan Powell. She'd miss him and his kisses. His humor and his way of life, but she knew that by staying here she was only fooling herself.

Her life was meant to take place somewhere else, and will and determination only went so far to change the course of one's life.

Seven

Evan soothed Jasmine with a bit of Scotch on her gums. The old-time doctor had diagnosed teething, and told Evan he often got panicked calls from first-time parents. Although modern medicine had come up with all sorts of rubs for a baby's gums, nothing worked better than a bit of Scotch. And since Placid Springs's only pharmacist closed his shop at 6:00 p.m. Evan's options were limited.

Jasmine finally stopped crying, her eyes blinking sleepily. His heart softened, seeing this little girl. She was so dependent on him.

Evan changed Jasmine and put her to bed. He needed to find Lydia. He didn't like the way she'd looked when she'd gone upstairs.

Closing Jasmine's door, he crossed the hall to find clothing strewn across Lydia's bed and half-full suitcases on the bed and chair. He'd avoided being upstairs with her since the evening when he'd lost control.

"What are you doing?" he asked.

"I've decided to leave." Her deep blue eyes were wide and tear-filled.

Evan wished he were the kind of man who had tender words to say. He wished he knew how to make her smile again. He wished life hadn't burnt all his softness out of him because he wanted to give those things to her.

"Why?"

Her hands trembled as she crumpled a silk shirt, tossing it in her suitcase. Her face was pale. For the first time since he'd met her, vitality didn't sparkle around her. His careless words meant to remind him to keep his distance had injured her.

"Jasmine shouldn't have to pay the price for my needing to find out who I am," she said. She turned her back on him and placed more clothing in her suitcase.

Didn't she know who she was? He left the question unasked because if he knew her even a bit better he wouldn't be able to keep his distance, and he needed to.

"She isn't."

"Yes she is. I heard her downstairs, Evan. Her entire day has been one big stress event."

He didn't know what to say to her. That she would doubt her abilities when she'd far outshone his expectations surprised him. He'd never understand women. And he'd never really know how to communicate with them. He always said the wrong thing.

"Sugar—"

"I'm going to take the Jeep and go to my aunt's house. I'll have someone return it with payment for my car."

Don't leave, he thought. But he wouldn't ask her to stay. He'd done that with Shanna. He'd bargained and begged, and in the end she'd left anyway. There was no way he was going to do that again.

"I thought your aunt was out of town."

She closed the latch on the suitcase on the bed and lifted the armload of remaining clothes to her other opened suitcase. "She is. I'll figure something out."

Evan realized there was nothing he could say to stop her. The only actions he had were frankly sensual in nature, and he knew she was vulnerable to him on that front. She'd as much as given herself to him the night before, and he wanted her that way again. But if she decided to stay, there had to be a better reason than sex.

"Lydia, if you want to leave I'm not going to stop you. But please don't leave because of what I said to you."

"Why not? You spoke the truth."

"The words weren't true." Damn, this was harder than he'd expected it to be.

"I find it hard to believe that you think I'm suddenly the maternal type."

"It has nothing to do with you," he said.

She just waited, letting the silence play out. Dammit, did everyone know his technique? He watched her calmly now, folding her clothing and then closing the last suitcase.

"You can't tell me more, can you?" she said slowly.

He stood there, afraid to say more and appear weak.

"I know why. It's because you believe it to be true. And you're partly right. I'm not the maternal type, but I've never felt more sure of myself than I did with Jasmine before today."

She started to leave the room, and he stopped her with his hand on her arm.

"Don't go."

"Give me a reason to stay."

"I can't."

She nodded. He was losing her, and he didn't know how to stop her.

"Lydia, I was married to a woman…who was from D.C., and she hated kids. You look a bit like her." God, he sounded like a moron.

Lydia didn't smile. "I thought we both agreed I wasn't your ex-wife."

"That doesn't mean you aren't like her in some ways. She hated kids. When one of them touched her she'd hold her body away so the baby wouldn't mess up her clothing or her hair."

"Am I like that?" she asked.

He remembered seeing her clothing caked with baby cereal and her hair loose around her shoulders. She was nothing like Shanna except in superficial ways. He knew he was going to have to give her the words she craved. But he'd talked more in the last few minutes than he'd ever done in the past with any woman.

He wanted to pull her against his chest so he wouldn't have to look her in the eye. Maybe that would make his words easier. Maybe then she wouldn't realize how vulnerable he was to her.

He settled for putting his hands on her shoulders and staring over head at the wall. Despite his fine plans, he pulled her close to him anyway.

"You are a wonderful mother to Jasmine, Lydia. You play with her and care for her. You've never once put yourself first, and I'm in awe of how much you've learned."

"Really?"

Holding her closely was having an effect on his body. Her high breasts nestled against his chest and her curves felt right under his hands. "Yes. Why do you doubt yourself?"

"You're so strong and sure of yourself you make me feel weak."

He pressed her hips against his manhood. "I'm not that strong."

Her expression changed and she rubbed against him. He loved the sensual way she moved when he held

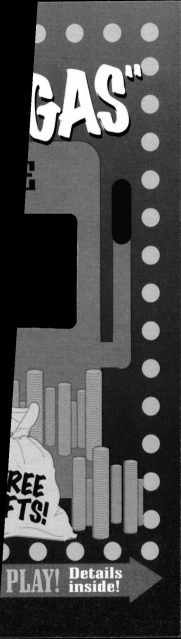

Play the

"LAS

3 FRE

FREE GIFTS!

1. Pull back all 3 tabs on the
   see what we have for you –
   FREE!

2. Send back this card and y
   novels. These books have
   $4.50 each in Canada, but

3. There's no catch. You're u
   nothing — ZERO — for y
   any minimum number of p

4. The fact is, thousands of re
   the Silhouette Reader Servic
   delivery...they like getting th
   they're available in stores...
   featuring author news, horos

5. We hope that after receiving
   subscriber. But the choice is
   all! So why not take us up on
   You'll be glad you did!

Play the
"LAS VEGAS"
Game

PEEL BACK HERE ▶
PEEL BACK HERE ▶
PEEL BACK HERE ▶

YES! I have pulled back the 3 tabs. Please send me all the free Silhouette Desire® books and the gift for which I qualify. I understand that I am under no obligation to purchase any books, as explained on the back and opposite page.

326 SDL DC47   **225 SDL DC42**
                                                    (S-D-OS-05/01)

NAME   (PLEASE PRINT CLEARLY)

ADDRESS

APT.#   CITY

STATE/PROV.   ZIP/POSTAL CODE

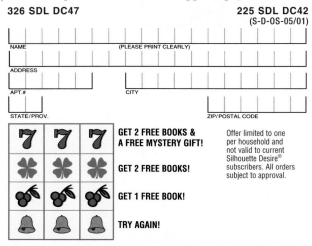

GET 2 FREE BOOKS & A FREE MYSTERY GIFT!

GET 2 FREE BOOKS!

GET 1 FREE BOOK!

TRY AGAIN!

Offer limited to one per household and not valid to current Silhouette Desire® subscribers. All orders subject to approval.

her. He wanted to feel her silky skin pressed against his. "Sure you are."

"Stop now if you're going to," he warned her.

"I'm not. Make love to me, Evan."

Her words went straight through him. It humbled him to think he affected her even a tenth as much as she affected him.

He lifted her in his arms and carried her the short distance to the bed. Settling her in the center of the mussed covers, he stood back and looked at the ice-blonde who wanted him. The ice-blonde who hadn't walked away from him. The ice-blonde who was the secret woman of his dreams.

Evan stood over her, the dark and mysterious lover who'd always claimed her dreams but never her real life. He was aroused, and his expression was almost harsh. This was no princely lover thinking of wooing a fair maiden. This was a real man with the desire to mate.

She reached up for him, longing for his mouth on her skin the way it had been last night. But he stood back. His eyes swept over her, igniting a firestorm of desire. Her blood pounded heavily in her veins, and her clothing irritated her skin.

She unbuttoned her blouse slowly, letting the edges fall away from her chest and revealing her creamy bra underneath. She knew her nipples were hard, could feel them against the lace demi-cups, but wanted to feel them surrounded by the heat of Evan's mouth.

He fell to his knees. His hands rubbing over her

torso, trembling slightly. His mouth sought hers, and he kissed her the way she'd always dreamed of being kissed by a man.

He touched her soul with kisses that said this man of few words felt deeply emotional about her. His hands caressed her breasts through her bra, and the stimulation was more than she could bear. She wanted to feel his flesh against hers.

She shrugged her shoulders, trying to wriggle out of her blouse but his touch moved, holding her shoulders to the bed. His palms were callused and hard, a working man's hands. His mouth left hers, skimming down her throat, letting her feel the edge of his teeth. Excitement and passion warred in her body.

He nipped gently at her aroused nipples and she moaned, arching her back so that he might take more of her nipple into his mouth. She wanted him to suckle her as he had the night before. She needed to feel the same connection she'd felt with him last night.

She wanted to feel like the bountiful earth mother to his wounded warrior. And he kept so many barriers between them during the day that this was the only time she experienced it. He actually needed her.

"Evan, take my blouse off…please."

"Not yet," he said. His voice was gruff and heavy. He stood and pulled his shirt over his head before unfastening his belt and removing his boots.

Evan blocked out the light coming from the overhead fixture, standing over her. He swept her shirt away and when she reached for the front clasp of her bra, he stopped her.

"Leave that for now, sugar."

She lay back on the fluffy pillow and watched him strip off his clothing. His chest was hard and lean with a thin line of hair tapering down into the waistband of his unfastened jeans. His skin was bronzed from working in the sun and his eyes were narrowed and intent.

When he shucked his jeans and underwear, she was taken aback by the sheer size of him. Moisture pooled at the center of her body, and she assured herself that this really would work.

He slid her shorts down her legs, leaving her covered in bikini panties and that damn bra. She squirmed a little, but he stilled her movements when he settled himself on the bed next to her.

He kissed her lips and neck. His hands caressed her head while he muttered softly in her ear, telling her things she'd never believed about herself. She was sexy and beautiful.

Her heart melted. She caressed her way down his chest around to his back. He felt warm, like the sun on a hot summer's day. She scored her fingernails down his back and heard him groan in response.

"Do you like that?" she asked, aware of her feminine power in that instant.

He grunted.

She slid her hands lower, caressing the firm cheeks of his buttocks. He slid closer to her, his body over hers now. She felt him hard and heavy at the center of her body. Her underwear was in the way.

His mouth left her neck, and he leaned back pressing his hard bulge into the heart of her. She moved her hips against him, delicious tingles spread throughout her body.

"Not yet, sugar."

She tried to still the movements of her hips, but he felt too good, she wanted more. He knelt between her thighs, reached down and removed her bra. She wondered if her pinkish nipples and small breasts would turn him off. But he fell to her. One hand cupping and lightly pinching one breast while his mouth suckled the other.

Here was what she'd been craving. She felt complete and whole in that moment. Like a woman who was attractive and lovely. Like a woman who could be the perfect mate for this man.

She grasped his head, holding him to her. He made her feel womanly, feminine. As if she were made for him and him alone in this moment.

His hand slid down between their bodies, pushing her panties down her legs. She kicked them free and felt the shock of warm skin to warm skin. Felt the incredible rightness of man and woman. Felt a drop of his moisture on her humid flesh.

His fingers tangled in the hair on her mound. His thumb rubbed intently at the nubbin at the top while he probed deep inside with first one then two fingers.

All the while his mouth worked at her breasts, alternating between them, arousing her to the flash point.

"Evan, please...now."

"Okay, sugar."

He rose up on his forearms, his eyes meeting hers. "Are you protected?"

"I'm on the pill."

He nodded and reached between their bodies once again. He positioned himself and slid into her in one smooth stroke. He broke past her body's barrier with ease, and Lydia felt free in a way she'd never felt before. She saw the questions in his eyes, but for once she was stronger.

She pulled his head to hers and claimed his mouth as he claimed her body. He thrust lightly into her. And used the hand between their bodies to stroke her into a frenzy.

She lifted her legs, locking her heels around his waist. Her hips lifted faster and faster. His thrusts became deeper and deeper.

She wanted more.

She needed more.

He gave her everything as she squeezed her eyes closed and the world exploded. A second later he thrust heavily and emptied himself into her body with a deep groan.

The air from the open window blew over them, and Lydia rubbed her hands up and down his back. His breathing was heavy and hers was just as ragged. She'd never imagined how intimate making love could be. Never thought her soul would leave her body and then return. Never thought she'd have to look her lover in the eye and explain why she'd been a virgin.

But looking into those frozen gray eyes, she knew she'd have to make just that explanation. She swallowed, not sure what to say.

"You should have held out for love, Lydia."

Hadn't he felt what she had?

"But I'm glad you didn't."

She snuggled closer to him and let the worries of tomorrow slip away. For right now, this was the perfect moment. And she realized now she could never marry for convenience because she'd felt the first tingles of love with this man. This man who would never fit into her real world.

The baby's cry woke Evan the next morning. Lydia climbed out of bed and donned her silk and satin robe. Evan watched her leave, wishing they'd had time to make love again.

Though he felt a certain sense of futility at his intimate relationship with her, he craved her in a way he'd craved nothing before in this life.

He stood and pulled on his jeans. He practiced Tae Kwon Do in the morning and evening usually, and he'd missed last night's session. He needed the grounding of martial arts now more than ever.

He scooped up the rest of his clothing, saw the small stain of blood on the bottom covers of Lydia's bed. He couldn't believe he'd been her first lover. But a part of his soul said it was rightly so. She'd been created for him and he for her. At least on the basic man-woman level.

He heard her talking softly to the baby as he entered the hallway, all of her doubts from last night gone. She was restored to the woman she'd been before the teething incident.

"Lydia?"

"Yes." Her hair was rumpled, her eyes sleepy and soft and he wanted nothing more than to go to her and claim her once again with his body.

"You're a great mother to Jasmine."

She nodded. And today he saw that she took his words for the praise they were. He knew they didn't make up for the hurting words he'd used before, but he hoped they'd heal her a little.

She leaned over to pick up the baby, and her robe gapped open. Her pretty breasts were revealed, and his body tightened in reaction. He wanted to seek nourishment from her again. She straightened and blushed as she realized where his gaze was on her body.

"Don't look at me like that in front of the baby."

"Do you really think she understands what I want from you?"

"No. Would you like to join us for breakfast?" she asked, suddenly shy.

"I have to work out. Maybe in thirty minutes?"

"Okay."

He walked away from her. For the first time he felt no freedom in the movement. It scared him in a way he'd never admit, but he felt he was protecting himself and didn't know why.

Eight

Though *Black Beauty* had been one of her favorite films as a little girl, Lydia found reality was a long way from fantasy.

The stable smelled of corn and hay. The light from a naked bulb cast a harsh illumination on the center aisle. Yet there was a sweetness to the night.

The air was warm and fragrant. She closed her eyes for a moment, forgetting the hulking animal next to her and enjoying the part of the experience she could. Evan had invited her to join him for a midnight ride. His dad was watching Jasmine, and she really wanted to spend time with Evan. She was excited about the ride. Well, would be if the horse wasn't part of the scenario.

She heard Evan moving quietly behind her, talking softly to his horse, which nickered back to him. She envied him his ease in this situation.

She still felt raw and vulnerable after making love to him the night before. And though he'd given her an experience that she wouldn't trade for the world, he'd also left her feeling unsure of who she was and what she wanted from life. He'd torn away the mask she'd always worn, and she wasn't sure he even realized it.

She knew that she wasn't a horsewoman. The big bay was eying her in the way she imagined a tiger watched a gazelle on the Serengeti that confirmed the knowledge was readily available to every creature in the barn.

''She's gentle.''

Startled, she turned toward Evan. He moved quietly for a big man. The shadow of his beard darkened his cheeks and he looked like a dusty hombre just in from many days on the range.

He looked tough and untameable, and she wondered for a moment if she wasn't in over her head. She fancied herself in a western dress with a whip in one hand. Ready to tame him and brand him as her own.

''She won't bite you,'' Evan said.

Yeah, right, she thought. They always said that until the horse went crazy. He must have taken her silence for fear, which it was. But a bigger part of her was frightened by the new feelings she felt toward Evan. He didn't seem like the kind of man who'd open his heart easily to love. And the feelings she had for him felt like love.

"I'm sure she is. It's just been a long time since I've ridden."

"How long?"

"Seventh grade and I wasn't that good at it."

He led his stallion out of the stall. She knew he was good as a sheriff but here in the barn with the horses he was in his element. There was an easiness to his movements, and a sense of rightness filled the air around them.

"I'm kind of an indoor gal."

"I know. But nothing beats a midnight ride."

She hesitated.

"Trust me, sugar."

She did, and that worried her because every other man she'd trusted had betrayed her. But Evan possessed a sureness that other men didn't. He was a man who wouldn't betray her. She hoped.

"Okay."

He helped her mount the horse and she sat on the top feeling like a bird perched nervously on a rhino's back. She smiled down at him the way she'd smiled at her father when she'd waved him off to work the day before she'd left town without a word. She hoped Evan was as easily fooled as her father had been.

"I won't let anything happen to you, Lydia," he said.

A warm feeling spread from her chest throughout her body. No one had ever offered her his protection before—not in this elemental way. Her father had tried to protect her by sending her to the best schools and training her to be a good wife. Her fiancé had tried to protect her by warning her not to look for hidden emotion in their marriage. But Evan was putting himself on the line.

She sensed beneath his words that he would do anything to keep her safe. And that moved her. She blinked back the tears that stung the back of her eyes and concentrated on staying on the horse. Don't think he could love you, she warned herself. He's already been burned once and is twice shy.

He mounted his own horse in a smooth powerful move and led the way out into the dark summer night. A warm breeze filled the air as she followed him. She closed her eyes and lifted her face toward it.

"Where are we going?" she asked after they'd been riding a few minutes.

"It's a surprise."

She smiled to herself, tickled that he'd planned something for her. His deep quiet voice made her feel like the only woman in the world who could share his secrets.

"Do you answer the front door in your towel often?"

"Only when a sexy blonde is on the other side."

"What if I'd been a redhead?"

"You would have missed out on a hell of a good thing."

She laughed. There were so many facets to Evan

that she had yet to explore fully. There was the deep caring he showed Jasmine. The respect and love he shared with his dad. His teasing and flirting with her and, of course, the deeper earthy level of his sensuality that permeated his lovemaking.

"What's that?" she asked, gesturing to a fenced-off area.

"The cemetery. My mom's buried up there with my grandparents and my great-grandparents."

She wanted to ask him more about the loss of his mom. She still missed hers, and every day without her had been so hard in the beginning. There was a sadness in Evan's voice that echoed the sadness in her own heart.

"When did your mom die?"

"When I was a senior in high school. My great-great grandparents homesteaded this land."

Obviously he didn't want to talk about his mother. "My great-greats left me a heritage too. But nothing like this."

"Yeah, this place is the best. They had to fight disease and every other hardship, but somehow they stuck together. Not many of today's couples would have survived back then."

"You don't think so?"

"Do you?"

"Well, I think when the stakes are raised we all make difficult decisions that normally wouldn't be within our comfort zone."

"Really?"

She'd forgotten he was a world-class flirt. Forgotten that he brought to the fore all the reactions she never had with other men. She'd forgotten he was a great temptation on every level.

"Yes, really."

"Do you have any proof of this, sugar?"

She gestured to herself. Trying desperately to keep the conversation on neutral ground because she didn't know if he thought this flirting would lead to love-making and her inexperienced body was too easily aroused.

"Look at me."

"I like to." The heat in his eyes told her that they'd be making love again. That once hadn't been enough for him either. She wondered if he'd felt that soul-deep connection that she had.

"I'm serious."

He raised one eyebrow and winked at her. "I am too."

She didn't think it was possible to be intimate with a man on a horse, but if he gave her one more of those heavy-lidded looks she was going to chance getting off Duchess and onto his horse.

"I mean circumstances that challenge us sometimes bring unexpected results."

"I'm sure they do."

She realized he didn't want to have any connections with her other than a sexual one and that bothered her. She reacted from the gut and said the first thing that came to mind.

"Do you honestly think I'd enjoy living here and taking care of a baby if I hadn't been totally desperate?"

He clicked to his horse and the animal stopped. Evan reached over and tugged on Duchess's reins.

His eyes were shuttered and cold, and she realized she'd gone too far. She had regretted the words as soon as they left her mouth because taking care of Jasmine and living in his house was exactly where she wanted to be in her life. Startled by the realization, she looked away.

"Are you desperate?"

"No," she said, carefully. She looked him straight in the eye. "I was angry."

"I know."

"No, you don't understand. I've always had men flirt with me and cosset me but never have they listened to my opinions and taken me seriously.

"You were teasing and I overreacted. I'm sorry."

He didn't say another word but dismounted and dropped the reins to his horse on the ground. "I should have given you more respect."

He lifted her down, letting her body brush against his until her feet were on the ground. She felt each exhalation of his breath as it caressed her face. "Where are we?"

"At the surprise."

"I'm definitely surprised."

"Close your eyes, sugar."

She did and he led her across some bumpy terrain,

lifting her into his arms when she stumbled. She opened her eyes and stared straight into his and felt the world tremble deep inside her.

Though he didn't say any words to her, she sensed that he'd needed to keep a distance between them. That his flirting was like a shield. Because in his eyes were the seeds of deep caring, and he didn't like it.

What had seemed like a great idea at the house was rapidly turning into the worst idea of his life, Evan thought. The small coquina cottage that his father's great-grandparents had settled had always felt more like home to him than the modern ranch house where he'd lived all his life.

He liked the one-room cottage with its stone fireplace and simple decor. But more than that he wanted to see Lydia there. To show her some of his past and how deeply connected he was to the land.

The woman in his arms was a tempting bundle. He knew she needed more than he had to give her. Even though she deserved a better man, one who could love her, he couldn't let her go.

Not now.

Later on, when her car was ready and it was time for her to leave, he'd watch silently. But tonight he needed her in an elemental way. Needed to make up for the silence and flirting he'd used to protect himself, in the process injuring her. There was something vulnerable about Lydia and that bothered him.

He wanted her to be the tough tiger that Shanna had

been. But at the same time he liked the innocence in her glances and the excitement of her touch.

"Can I open my eyes now?" she asked. Her voice wasn't uncertain or scared, and he realized that she trusted him. He'd invited her to do so, but knowing that she did touched him in a way he hadn't been in a long, long time.

"No."

He shifted her in his grasp and opened the door to the cottage. He set her on her feet. "Keep your eyes closed."

He lit the lamp he'd left there earlier and then went to stand behind her. He wanted to wrap his arms around her and hold her to him in a strong embrace. He wanted to strip her jeans and silk shirt from her body and revel in the awe that this soft sexy woman was his. At least for the present.

"Open your eyes, sugar," he said.

The old hardwood floors were covered in a soft pile of blankets, and there was a picnic basket. He'd laid some wood in the fireplace and now went to ignite it. The wine he'd left chilling in the ice bucket was an expensive bottle he'd been given when he'd been re-elected sheriff.

Glancing over his shoulder at Lydia he wondered at her silence. A sheen of tears glistened in her eyes. Ah, hell. What had he been thinking? He should have known better than to try to pull off something this romantic.

He wasn't a romance kind of guy. He was much

better at spontaneous lovemaking than pre-planning. Give him a rowdy horse or temperamental steer and he had no troubles. But give him a city woman and the situation always went straight to hell.

"We can leave." He'd wanted to give her something special because he knew he wasn't the kind of guy who could give her the words she needed. And she'd given him the special gift of being her first man. To a lot of women it was no big deal, virginity being more of a bother than a restraint, but Lydia was different.

"No way."

He glanced back at her.

"I..."

She walked slowly toward him, her fingers loosening the buttons on her blouse. Her hair flowed free around her shoulders, and he longed to bury his fingers in her tresses. Longed to finish opening the buttons on her blouse. Longed to bury himself to the hilt in that feminine body of hers.

Leaning up on her toes, she took his face in her hands, her grip firm but gentle, her eyes wide and caring, her lips warm and exciting. She kissed him all the way to his toes.

"Thank you."

He didn't want her thanks. Had wanted this whole night to be her fantasy, but couldn't say the words. He didn't know what her fantasy was, but he knew women liked candlelight and wine and flowers. Damn, he'd forgotten the flowers.

"Don't thank me yet," he said.

"I'll thank you again," she said, with a distinct gleam in her eyes.

He wanted to forget the niceties of seduction and mate with her like the primal man he was. But he'd gone to a lot of trouble to set this whole thing up.

"Would you like a glass of wine?"

"Yes, please."

"Have a seat," he said and went to open the bottle. He poured two glasses of Chardonnay and turned toward the blanket. Lydia leaned back on her elbows. The firelight made her blond hair shine. He felt as if he'd taken a punch to the gut. She was so beautiful to him.

He set the glasses on the mantel and returned to her empty-handed. He needed her now. He realized that his evening of seduction had been turned around on him. He was now thoroughly seduced by her.

He dropped to his knees beside her, thrust his hands in her hair and pulled her to him. His tongue thrust deep into the recesses of her mouth, tasting more than woman—the very essence of life.

He slid his hands inside her unbuttoned shirt, searching for her nipples, needing to bring her to the same flash point of arousal that he was already at. His erection strained against his jeans.

Her hands slid from his shoulders down his chest before burrowing under the back of his shirt. He felt the bite of her nails as she pressed her torso against his. He left her mouth, biting his way down her neck, stopping to suckle her left breast through the barrier of her clothing.

"Let me take your shirt off," she said.

He ripped the garment off and tossed it across the room. Her shirt and bra followed quickly. Slow down, he told himself.

He urged her to lie flat on her back and removed her jeans with hands that trembled. The white lace underpants she wore were a red flag to his already raging hormones. He skimmed his hands across her body. He followed the silky line of her legs down to her toes and then back up the inside, stopping only when he felt the humid warmth of her feminine mound. He slid one finger inside the leg of her panties.

She moaned and lifted her hips toward him. He pulled the scrap of lace down her legs and bent, kissing her where she was most a woman. She drew back.

"Evan..." her hands tightening in his hair, keeping him from continuing.

"Let me do this, sugar."

It wasn't something he'd done with other women, but he wanted to have the taste of her so firmly imbedded in himself that he missed it when she wasn't there. He wanted to do the same to her. Her hands fell to his shoulders and he moved forward.

He parted the lips of her sex and bent to taste her heart. She moaned again and carefully he used his teeth and tongue to bring her to the pinnacle of her desire. She writhed on the blanket, her thighs parting wider to give him greater access.

She screamed as her orgasm overcame her, and Evan slid up her body taking her cries into his mouth, thrusting his tongue deep in her throat. She pulled back from him.

"I want to taste you, too."

He ignored her words, intent on pleasuring her. His own skin felt too tight—as if he would combust at any moment. He felt her long, cool fingers open his button fly and then slip inside his briefs.

"I'm not going to last if you keep that up."

"That's the idea."

She pushed his underwear out of the way, freeing him, and stared down at his body. Next to her fragile frame he felt like a big hulking brute, too big and tough for her. But she leaned down and brushed a kiss against his hot, longing flesh.

Suddenly he couldn't wait any longer. A drop escaped his control, and Lydia licked it from his body. He pushed her back against the blanket. Her eyes widened as he folded her legs back toward her body and thrust into her without waiting another moment.

He felt her body resist him and then accept him. Felt her hands in his hair and her mouth along his neck. Her nails scraped down his back, and she whimpered deep in her throat.

"Come on, sugar, take more of me."

Her body softened even more, and he slid hilt-deep into the hot welcome of her. He felt as if he were sliding into her soul. Her eyes never left his, and something changed profoundly inside him. Her body clenched around his, and the tingle of orgasm rippled through his body. Her eyes rolled back, and she moaned loud and long.

He knew that she was his. In that moment he knew that she was meant to be his for all time and he didn't know how he was going to keep her from leaving.

Nine

The next morning Lydia felt like an imposter. Or a fairy-tale princess the morning after the prince rescues her, and she realizes that reality isn't necessarily the pretty vision that happily-ever-after promised.

Jasmine was happily chewing on her teething ring and now that Lydia had found a teething gel, life in their house was calm. Payne was teaching her to whittle and telling her about Florida history. Evan had invited her and the baby to join him for lunch.

She was happy in the way only someone who was between existences could be. She knew that what she was doing in her daily life wasn't reality.

Couldn't be. Her father and Manhattan were her life. Yet she was content to stay at the Powell home and play with the baby.

She'd driven into town and checked on her car, which was almost finished. The bodywork was complete, but the engine still needed one part. Boz had grumbled that it had taken more time and money than totaling the car, but when she'd praised his work, he'd stood up straighter and pride had shone from him, despite his dirty overalls.

The Pine Street Diner was packed and Lydia balanced the baby on her hip, scanning the crowd for Evan. He saw her and waved. She made her way through the crowded room slowly. Everyone marveled over how big Jasmine was getting and how pretty she was.

"Hello," Evan said as she sat down. She wanted to lean across the table and kiss him, but figured he wouldn't appreciate a public display of affection in front of his hometown folks. Besides there was something very small-town and charming about Placid Springs, and she wanted to be a part of it.

"Any word on Jasmine's parents?" Lydia asked.

"I've got a line on a girl who disappeared with her baby about the same time Jasmine showed up."

He took the baby from her and settled her in a high chair. Jasmine grinned up at him, a little bit of drool running down her cheek. Her brown eyes were wide and focused on Evan.

"Damn if she isn't the cutest little thing," he said.

Her heart ached because she realized that she couldn't stay here. She'd never fit into small-town living the way that Jasmine and Evan did. In a couple of weeks her car would be ready and she'd be leaving the only man who'd ever made her feel really alive.

"I bet you think all girls who drool are cute."

Scratching his chin, he said, "To be honest, it's what drew me to you."

"Ha ha."

"That and your quick thinking with comebacks."

Lydia smiled to herself and pretended to read the menu. In some ways she fit just fine in Placid Springs. Unfortunately she couldn't spend twenty-four hours a day with Evan.

The waitress took their order and brought their drinks. A strange silence fell between them. Lydia wondered if he was remembering last night and the firelight. The raw beauty of their joining and the emotions that still were unsettled.

In fact, she'd been unable to think of anything else all morning. How could a man who professed not to be able to love use his body to touch her soul?

"Penny for your thoughts?" he said.

Not even a million would tempt her to reveal them. She knew he wanted more than lust and less than love from her. But suddenly that arrangement didn't work.

It really never had. She wanted every damn thing he had to give her. And she wanted it for more than the next few weeks.

"Just daydreaming."

"About...?" He leaned forward, the scent of his aftershave surrounded her. His silver-gray eyes narrowed, and she felt his touch like a velvet glove on her body.

She blushed. "Something that can never be."

He glanced away, and she knew she'd said too much, although she really felt she'd said too little. She wished she'd kept her mouth shut.

"Boy, it's hot today," she said.

"Yeah, but it's not the heat that gets to you, it's the humidity."

"Well that's stimulating. Shall we talk about the rain chances for this afternoon or just let a polite silence fall?"

"Dammit, Lydia—"

"Yes, dammit. Don't ask me questions you don't want answered."

Silence fell, and she let it stretch between them. She didn't want to discuss the weather any more than he did. She wanted to curl in a ball and find her defenses, the ones he'd blasted right through without even realizing it.

"I invited you to lunch for a reason," he said, quietly.

"Yes?" She was almost afraid to ask why.

"The Junior Women's Club would like for you to speak to them."

She was flattered. "What about?"

"Fashion and clothing."

It was the one thing she always fell back on. "I'd love to."

He cleared his throat. "They meet on Thursday evenings. I have to work this week, but maybe my dad can watch the baby.''

"Sounds good to me.''

Their food arrived and they both ate, but there was still a tension at the table. The baby gummed her teething cookie, and they both took turns staring at the baby or out the window.

It was a relief when she finished eating and could easily get up and leave. "Well, thanks for lunch.''

She wiped the baby's face and began to gather her purse and the diaper bag. Evan stood when she did and lifted the baby from the seat, handing her to Lydia.

She started to leave but his hand on her arm held her in place. "I wish I could offer you more.''

The words confirmed what she knew. "I know—more than lust, less than love.''

"I'm just not programmed for love, Lydia.''

"I don't believe that. We are all programmed for love.''

"But some of us believe it's not worth the pain.''

"Do you?''

He didn't say anything else but dropped his hand from her arm. "You're the one who's always walking away.''

Evan tossed some bills on the table and walked out of the diner. Lydia watched him leave. She *did* always walk away. It was easier than watching everyone else leave. She realized that she was afraid that Evan was going to retreat from her before she could leave herself.

* * *

Evan focused inwardly, performing the eighth form in Tae Kwon Do. He imagined an adversary in the room with him and took out all of his pent-up frustration on him. Images of Lydia lurked in the back of his mind.

It had been a week since their disastrous lunch. What he really needed was full-contact sparring, but there wasn't a black belt in Placid Springs, and he couldn't drive to West Palm Beach to spar with his regular partner because of his work schedule.

Thick tension permeated the air in the ranch house and whenever he entered a room, Lydia found an excuse to exit. Most of her excuses were damn flimsy too. He knew that he was to blame. He shouldn't have been so blunt, but he wasn't a man to whom social niceties came easily.

He ended the form with a ruthless middle punch that would have cut down even the toughest street hood, and found his blood pumping more chaotically than before. Someone cleared their throat, and he didn't turn to see who it was.

He knew that Lydia stood in the doorway of his workout room. His skin tingled, and blood rushed to his groin. He burned to have her again, but there was a distance between them that he couldn't bridge. Soft words would do the trick but they'd never come easily to him.

He knew that she'd have some sort of vague expression in her eyes that masked her true feelings.

Knew that if he did pivot to face her, he wouldn't stop at just looking. The only time they really communicated was when they were both naked and he was hilt-deep in her body.

"Can we talk?" she asked, her voice soft and husky, reminding him of their last night together.

He bent to pick up his towel and slung it around his neck, wiping the sweat from his forehead. "Sure."

He heard her walk across the room and settle on the bench of his weight machine. He turned to face her. She was breathtakingly lovely, and, for a woman on the run, she seemed to be more at ease than he.

"I've been asked to help out at the unwed mothers' home three days a week. I'd like to tell them yes, but that would commit you to watching Jasmine."

For a woman who'd been unable to answer the phone in his office with any skill, she really had a gift for interacting with people. Shanna had never wanted to do anything in Placid Springs. In fact, he'd been surprised when Lydia had agreed to talk to the Junior Women's Club. But Shanna and Lydia were eons apart. Which is why it was so hard to resist her.

"No problem. The Baptist Church has a day-care center. In fact, once your car's ready and you leave, I'm planning to take the baby there."

Lydia hugged her arms around her waist, looking fragile and uncertain. "Any word on her mother or father?"

"Not enough. I feel like we're close to tracking her

down. You might ask around at the center and see if any of the women knew her.''

''I will.''

''Was that all?'' he asked. He needed her out of his sanctuary. This was the one room in the house that held no memories of her, and he liked it that way. It was his retreat from duty and responsibility, and now she'd invaded it. He needed to be able to find some peace, and he couldn't while she was there.

''I guess so.'' She stood but didn't move.

''I hate this awkwardness between us. I miss talking to you.''

Me too. But he wouldn't tell her. He was already too vulnerable where she was concerned.

She moved slowly toward him, stopping well within his reach and he wanted to pull her even closer. To wrap her in his arms until they were fused together and she lived in his soul. Wait a minute, he thought. She wasn't going to stay. Placid Springs and you, old son, aren't what she needs.

''What do you want from me, Lydia?'' he asked.

''I don't know. More than we've had the past week.''

''You're the one who's leaving.''

''I know. But I'm not sure I want to.''

''I'm not the kind of man to offer you soft words and promises, but if you did stay I'd like for you to be my lover.''

''What about love?''

''I told you, it's not in my programming.''

"Why not?"

"Maybe it's the way I was raised."

"There's more to it than that."

"How can you be sure?"

"Because the stoic cowboy is a stereotypical man, and you're a three-dimensional man."

"Sometimes it's easier to be stereotypical."

"I know."

"How do you know?"

"Hey, I'm the socialite with the icy-cool looks. Nothing but the best clothes, cars and men."

"Why would you stay here?"

"I'm more than a socialite."

"Yes, you are."

"Then it follows you must be more than a stoic cowboy."

He knew what she wanted from him. But gut instinct stopped him. "I tried it your way once, and as much as I wanted it to work, it didn't."

"I don't understand."

"I can't be the nine-to-five, lawn-mowing man next door, Lydia. My marriage broke up for a couple of reasons. One of them was that Shanna and I both thought we had to pretend to be in love."

"Why pretend?"

"Because love doesn't exist."

He stopped her argument with a finger across her lips.

"It's just a pretty lie that men and women tell each

other to convince themselves that sacrificing their dreams is worthwhile.''

She tilted her head and stared up at him, her wide blue eyes making him feel as if she were probing past his defenses and finding the heart he'd hidden deep within his soul. ''Love is never a lie. Does your dad lie to you?''

''No, but then he doesn't say he loves me.''

''But you know he does, right?''

''How do I know? Our relationship is based on mutual respect and friendship.''

''There's more to it than that.''

''No there isn't. Only women worry about love. Men are more comfortable with the facts.''

''Are you saying all women are deluding themselves?''

''No. But they do always need to label relationships as either lust or love.''

''You did the same thing.''

''Yes, but I knew that love didn't exist, and that a city woman would never stay in this small town.''

''Not when you keep driving her away.''

''I'm not. I'm just being realistic.''

She grasped both ends of his towel and tugged, bringing his face level with hers. ''I challenge you.''

''To what?''

''To put those outdated notions aside and see the *reality* in front of you.''

''What reality?''

"Affection and caring and a family. Or are you too afraid?"

"I'm not afraid of any woman," he said, though he knew the words were a lie.

"Then we're on."

"I'm not sure what this bet is."

"I'm going to show you that love is more than pretty words."

"And if you don't."

"Then I'll be the one to lose." She turned and walked away.

He watched her go, feeling as though he'd just condemned them both to purgatory, but not knowing what else to do. He wanted the glimpse of heaven she'd offered him, even if he'd have to spend eternity in hell to pay the price.

Lydia's car was still with the mechanic due to a mix-up at the manufacturer. They'd shipped the wrong part. Lydia didn't regret it. She wasn't in a hurry to leave Placid Springs, and she had the feeling that Evan was going to push her away as soon as she had transportation.

She found a new strength in herself over those few weeks. Her days were busier than they'd ever been in the past. People depended on her for things other than a charitable donation, and at first that had scared her. But lately it seemed almost to strengthen her. She felt as if she were becoming the woman her mother would have wanted her to be.

She was volunteering three afternoons a week and found the work both rewarding and challenging. The Women's Center had badly needed someone to help the unwed teenage mothers build their self-esteem. Lydia had been surprised to find the girls responding to her lessons in fashion and makeup.

The teen mothers in the center admired her clothes and style, but were reluctant to share any information with her. She'd taught them all some simple tips she'd learned as a young girl watching her model mother work, and the girls now had a new confidence in themselves simply from changing the way they looked.

Jasmine was always so happy to see her at the end of the day that Lydia wondered how she'd survive once the baby was returned to her mother. She really missed the baby while they were apart. It shook her to realize how deep the temporary roots she'd put down were growing.

"See you next week, Lydia," Charlotte, the woman who ran the girls' shelter, said as Lydia left the building. Lydia liked Charlotte. She had a tough but caring way about her that made all the teen mothers both respect and love her. They all knew she'd go to the wall for them in any battle, but that she demanded and got total honesty.

She missed her father. She'd left another message for him but now her reasons for not talking to him had changed. Now she didn't want her dream world to end. She'd never thought she'd have to resort to such desperate measures, since the two of them were all that

each other had in the world. Lydia had to admit,
though, she was finding a new happiness and sense of
belonging with Evan and Jasmine. She wished her father could be a part of it, but he'd never approve of
Evan as a husband for her. Did his opinion still matter?
she wondered as she spotted Evan.

He was leaning against the side of his truck, waiting
for her. His faded jeans and button-down shirt would
have looked casual on any other man, but they were
like a second layer of skin on him, accentuating his
lean legs and muscular chest. Her pulse quickened,
and she hurried her steps across the parking lot.

They'd been working together in an uneasy truce.
She'd been showering him with affection and had con-
vinced him to pick the baby up from day care every
afternoon before coming to get her from the center. It
gave them a chance to be a family, which, in her heart,
was what Lydia wanted.

They hadn't slept together since that night in his old
family cottage. It was torture to see him every day. To
prepare meals, shop for groceries and ride to work
together and feel alone. He never held any conversations with her and now had taken to having his meals
before he came home.

She sensed he tried to keep her at arm's length and
the friendship they were building was all he could give
her. Or all he was comfortable giving her. But she
longed to feel his strong arms around her in the middle
of the night. She ached to be his again in the most
primal sense. Tonight she aimed to do something

about it, but Evan was her first lover, and she didn't really know how to bridge the gap between them.

To that end she'd borrowed an issue of *Cosmopolitan* from the Home. The cover bragged that the magazine held the key to "Keeping Your Man Satisfied." She hoped it was detailed.

Jasmine was in his arms, chewing on his collar. His head was lowered next to the baby's, and she heard the low rasp of his voice. That baby was trying so hard to get her teeth in!

Lydia smiled at them as she hurried across the parking lot. The summer sun dipped low in the sky and it was still hot. She lifted her face toward the warm breeze, feeling alive in a way she'd never felt before.

She brushed a kiss on Jasmine's cheek and the baby stopped chewing long enough to look at her. The scent of baby lotion and strawberries assailed her. She wanted to hold the baby to her chest and hug her as tight as she could.

She took the baby from Evan and waited for him to open the door for her so she could secure the baby. Then he opened her door and helped her in, his hand lingering at her elbow. She grabbed his arm before he could move away, caressing him.

"Lydia," he said.

"What?"

"I'm holding on to my control by a thread."

"Don't hold on to it on my account."

He watched her like a hawk with a field mouse in

its sights. "I know you're the type of woman who falls in love easily."

She wondered how he knew that, because, unless she was mistaken, this was the first time she'd even come close to love. "Please—not another comparison to your ex-wife."

"You're nothing like her," he said. He cupped her face in his hands and leaned down, brushing the softest kiss against her cheek.

"Evan, you confuse me."

"I confuse myself sometimes. But I don't want to hurt you."

"You won't."

"I know I will. Please let me protect you."

How could one person protect another from heartbreak? There was no way. Yet that was what he wanted to do.

"I have some news."

"About Jasmine's mother?"

"No. HRS has a foster family ready to take over care of her."

No, Lydia wanted to scream. It was too soon. She wasn't ready to stop being a mom. "When?"

"Next week."

"Really?" she asked, having expected to have to drop the baby off somewhere on the way home.

"They're ready now, but I knew you wouldn't be."

Lydia felt tears stinging the back of her eyes. "I'm not ever going to be. Oh, Evan, what are we going to do?"

He was quiet for a moment.

"The right thing."

"The right thing would be for us to keep her."

"We're not married."

"I know. I don't think we have to be."

"Maybe not in whatever big city you're from but in Placid Springs, Florida, you have to be."

"We're her family."

"We're public servants, Lydia."

"I'm not."

He was quiet as he started the truck and backed out of the parking space. "You knew she'd be leaving. It was only a question of which one of you would go first."

His words tore through her, and she realized that the stoic cowboy had been trying to protect himself. And if his words were any indication, he hadn't done a very good job.

She reached across the seat and took his hand in hers. He clung tightly to her, and she felt like the strong one. It felt good. A ray of sunshine in the storm brewing around them. Her heart overflowed with emotion, and she knew in an instant that she loved him.

Ten

Evan stood at the fence watching the stars in the night sky. He'd never expected to grow to care for Jasmine or Lydia, but he'd been startled to find tonight that he did. It was harder than he'd expected as well to realize that he hadn't done any better job of preparing himself this time than he had when Shanna left.

If anything, he hurt worse.

"You okay, son?"

"Yeah, Dad."

His father joined him at the fence, one booted foot on the bottom rung. A cigarette burned in his left hand, he took a deep drag and then coughed.

"These things are going to kill me one day," Payne said.

It shook Evan to think of his dad gone. "You should quit."

Payne just nodded. His dad looked old, and his shoulders were beginning to stoop a little. Where had the strong cowboy from his childhood gone? It bothered him to realize that years were slipping by, and he hadn't been paying attention.

"Lydia mentioned the baby is leaving."

"HRS found a foster home for her," Evan said.

"I really like that little girl, but it will be better for her to be in a permanent home."

He admired his father's attitude, and wished his could be the same, but it wasn't. The cycles of life had always seemed out of control. As a child he'd hated having livestock for eating on the ranch. He'd set more pigs, turkeys and chickens free until his dad had caught on and stopped raising them to eat. He knew it wasn't only lack of control that motivated him. He hated to lose a pet or a friend.

Uncomfortable with his own thoughts, he tried to direct his dad's attention elsewhere. He wasn't up to another discussion on how he wanted grandkids. Not tonight, when all he could think about was his dad's mortality and Jasmine leaving. Lydia wouldn't be far behind and he'd be alone again.

"Lydia's taking it hard."

"That little gal would. She's spent the most time with the baby."

He wanted to go to her. To wrap her in his arms and tell her that he'd protect her from the hurts in the world but knew he couldn't. There were some things you just couldn't hide from.

"You think any more about what I said?"

"About what, Dad?"

"My grandchildren."

"Hell, no."

Payne turned toward the barn but then stopped. "I'd stop smoking if you'd get serious about finding a wife and having some babies."

Evan watched his father leave, figuring that the crusty old coot would outlive him. Payne Powell was too stubborn to leave this earth until he'd browbeaten his son into settling down again.

Evan headed for the house. Heat lightning split the sky, and he watched Mother Nature's light show. He made it as far as the porch and decided he wasn't ready to go inside. He didn't want to see Jasmine's toys on the living-room floor or her bottles next to the sink in the kitchen.

A lullaby drifted from the upstairs window. Lydia's voice crooning softly to the baby. She'd done good, his city girl. Better than anyone had a right to expect her to.

Certainly better than he'd expected. But then it wouldn't have taken a lot to beat his expectations. Evan was the first to admit that at times he could be a bit of a cynic, but he figured that didn't excuse him for the way he'd treated Lydia.

Time and again it seemed he'd led her right smack into a situation beyond her experience and then watched her flounder. It never occurred to him that she'd become as attached to the baby as she had. Probably because he'd never looked behind the mask she presented to the world to the woman underneath.

Though she was the one person he never wanted to hurt, he was fairly certain he'd hurt her more than once.

Using all the stealth he'd acquired in his training with the FBI and over fifteen years in law enforcement, he crept into the house and up the stairs. He froze in the hallway, afraid, yes dammit, afraid, to go any further. In the deepest recesses of his soul he knew what he longed for.

It was more than a sweet sexy woman in his bed at night. It was more than a successful ranch and a peaceful quiet town. As he stood in the doorway of the converted guest room, he acknowledged that it was a family.

This family?

He shied away from answering that question. He'd faced enough ghosts tonight without battling any more.

Jasmine stared at him from over Lydia's shoulder.

"Da..da..da," Jasmine said.

Lydia pivoted to face him, her eyes wide and a huge smile on her face. "Did you hear that?"

Yes, he thought. "It's just babbling. All babies do it."

She held the baby closer and dropped a kiss on her head. "You're right."

She placed Jasmine in her crib and wrapped her snugly in a light blanket before backing out of the room. The light in the hall made her blond hair come alive like something out of a fairy tale. If he were a poet he'd be able to liken it to something that gave it justice. Instead all he could think was that it was light and soft, much like the first rays of dawn over the horizon.

"You doing okay?"

"I could use a hug."

He opened his arms and let her step into them. She nestled closer, resting her head right over his heart. The damn organ skipped a beat.

"I don't want to give her up."

He rubbed her back trying to think of the right words to say but there weren't any. At least not any that he knew. He felt the wetness of her tears soaking his shirt and hugged her even closer. God, he didn't know how he was going to face the silence when Lydia left.

Standing in Evan's arms made her feel as if she'd found her home. She knew she'd have to make a decision about her future. It felt like time was running out. Moving on no longer seemed like the thing to do.

In fact, running away from her dad didn't look too smart in retrospect. At the time she couldn't have taken any other action, but now she wished she'd stood up for herself in the first place. She didn't regret leaving Manhattan because if she hadn't, she wouldn't have met Evan and Jasmine.

She rubbed her nose, wishing for a tissue. A snowy white handkerchief appeared at eye level and she leaned back in Evan's arms to delicately blow her nose. She wished she was the kind of lady who could cry gracefully, like her mom had, but her face always turned splotchy.

She buried her face in his shoulder again, not wanting him to see her with her defenses lowered. At this moment she wasn't sure who she was. She envied Evan his strength and self-assurance. Maybe if she stayed close enough to him some of it would rub off.

But she knew that he didn't want the baby to go either; had felt it in the force of his grip earlier in the car. It was also evident in the firm set of his jaw and the icy expression in his eyes.

His hands on her back continued to rub, and she pocketed the handkerchief. For today she wanted to let him shoulder this burden. But not alone. She knew she could never be a full partner with Evan unless he loved her and that was something he didn't believe he could do.

He needed someone to be his strength. She'd tried to do it earlier in the truck but now when the chips were down and reality was yawning in front of her like a black hole ready to swallow a small planet, she was quivering. Her plans had backfired, she realized.

She'd forced Evan to interact with both her and the baby, hoping they'd form a family unit. Never had she thought of the price they'd pay when Jasmine had to leave.

She sniffled again.

He murmured soft words against her ear. She couldn't understand his words, but her heart melted. She loved him.

Evan was comforting her by offering her the one thing she really needed—human closeness. She wanted to tell him that he wasn't living up to his ideal of the stoic cowboy, but her heart wasn't up to bantering with him. Besides it seemed one or both of them always left those encounters with wounds gaping in their psyches.

Leaning up, she kissed him. She loved his mouth firm and hard, sensual and warm. His arms didn't move, but he rocked back, letting the wall support him and her feet left the ground.

She moaned, tilting her head to the side, taking control of the kiss. He'd given her the freedom to be in command because she had nothing to worry about in this moment. She desperately wanted to forget about the myriad of worries facing them.

The rock-hard strength of his right arm supported her while his other arm caressed her back. She held him tighter, tasting the essence of man and memorizing it. Taking that knowledge to the seat of her soul so she'd be able to pull it out and remember when he'd shut her away again.

It hurt her to know that he wasn't going to change into the kind of man she'd like him to be. A safe man who'd do as she bid him to do and take her dad's money. Instead she had to fall in love with a man with a sharp definition of who he was and the strength of character to walk away from someone even if he cared for her, if that was the right thing to do.

She pulled back, gasping for air. Watching him let Jasmine go had hammered home a few solid truths. The quiet, calm way he'd handled the whole delivery of the news and the subsequent hours showed her exactly how he'd act when she left. Did she mean anything to him? His touch said she did but what did that mean?

Lust not love.

He set her on her feet. She knew the embrace had affected him as much as it had her—could see the physical proof in the hard ridge pressing against his fly. She wanted to lead him into her bedroom and make love to him for the rest of the night.

"You okay, now?"

"I will be. I'm sorry for falling apart like that," she said softly.

"That's okay. You're not an expert on this end."

She wasn't sure what he meant, and didn't know that she wanted to be sure. "What day does Jasmine have to be at the new home?"

"Monday."

"Well at least we have the weekend. Let's do something fun with her. Just the three of us."

"No."

"Why not?"

"Why? What purpose would it serve for us to spend more time with her? She's leaving, Lydia."

She saw the stoic cowboy he'd said he wanted to be. He was closed off emotionally from her and the baby at that moment. There was nothing in the world that was going to change his mind and make him spend more time with them.

"I like the thought of us being a family."

"Me too. But it isn't reality."

"Would it be so bad if it was?"

"Why wish for things that can't come true?"

"You're not that cynical."

"Yes, I am."

He started to walk away and Lydia touched his arm to stop him. "You're not alone in this."

"I will be soon enough."

She waited, sensing there was more he had to say by the way he stared at her.

"Sooner or later you're going to leave. Right now, missing Jasmine hurts and hurts you bad. But that's only because you've never been on this side of the action before."

He shrugged out of her grip and she watched him leave, knowing he was right. How could she expect him to want her to stay when she didn't know if she wanted to? How could she expect him to leap when she was afraid to? How could she leave when staying here might bring her the happiness she'd always wanted in her heart?

Evan felt like a bear who'd been trapped by his own stupidity. He'd pulled a double shift over the weekend and now he had to go to the courthouse to meet Lydia and Jasmine and then turn the baby over to Family Services.

The phone rang, and he barked out his name. There was silence for an answer. Then the delicate clearing of a feminine throat.

"Evan?"

"Yes, Lydia."

"Are you okay?" He liked that she cared enough about him to ask.

Don't let it mean too much, he told himself. "I'm fine. What do you want?"

"Can I stop by the station and drop Jasmine off with you? I don't really want to…"

He heard a sniffle on the other end and wished she were here so he could wrap his arms around her and comfort her. He wouldn't have thought it possible but her pain was his. And it was very deep, he realized. All the way to his soul.

"Sure, sugar. Bring the baby by."

"Thanks," she said and hung up.

His skin felt too tight for his body. He'd never felt this way about anyone before, and it bothered him. He shouldn't care that a baby temporarily in his care was going to be placed in Child Welfare Services. He shouldn't be affected by the loss of the laughter and noise at the ranch house. He shouldn't care that the young woman he was involved with didn't want to give up the baby. But he did.

He'd never realized that a woman like Lydia could

love a baby. He knew her well enough to know that she thought she loved the child. Even knowing the situation wouldn't last, she'd allowed herself to be vulnerable in a way he never would have.

Everyone in the station house was ready to see him leave for the day. Deputy Hobbs was finally developing a backbone and had mildly inquired if Evan needed to go to the gym and work out some of his frustration. Offered to spar with him if need be. Evan was ready to take him up on the offer when the receptionist told him there was someone to see him.

The young woman who sat in his guest chair looked maybe fifteen. Her hair was long and dyed jet black, she had piercings in her lip, nose and eyebrow. Dressed entirely in fatigues, she looked like the survivor of a bloody battle. She watched him with eyes that were the same color as Lydia's but didn't have that sweet innocence. Instead they were weary.

"Hello, miss. I'm Sheriff Powell. What can I do for you?" he asked.

"I'm Eden Lavene. I…uh…Sheriff…"

"Yes."

She looked at her combat boots and twirled the strap on her book bag but didn't answer him. He wondered if she had trouble with a boyfriend using drugs. A lot of teens did. It took courage to come to visit him.

"Whatever it is, I'm here to help," he said.

"I know," she said softly, her voice barely audible. "I left my baby at your house."

He sat back, absorbing what she'd said. Well, this

was interesting. The mother returns just days after HRS finally intercedes. *Well, pardon me if I'm cynical,* he thought.

"And now you want her back." He'd seen it a hundred times. But there was no way the courts were going to give the baby back to this girl until she cleaned up her act. Hell, he'd intercede if he had to, because the baby girl he'd come to care for wasn't going to end up looking like this at fifteen. Not while there was a breath in his body.

"No. I want you to keep her."

"That's not the way the system works."

"I grew up in the system. Not here but I wanted better for my Jasmine."

"Kid, you don't know me from Adam."

"Yeah I do. I've been watching your place. And one of my friends has met your wife at the women's center."

Great. He must be slipping not to have noticed this girl snooping around his place. "When?"

"Mostly during the day when you're not around. I mean you're a tough-looking guy, and I worried about Jasmine when I first got a look at you, but then I watched your wife with Jasmine. She's way better than I ever was at being a mother. I just know my baby will have a better chance in life if you raise her. Please?"

Evan leaned back in his chair, floored by the thought of Lydia as his wife. To legally have a claim on her was something he hadn't realized he'd been missing. He hadn't thought about that before, but it was the perfect solution.

Of course, she'd have to wrap up the loose ends with her family. Maybe he should look into that. Find out just what she was running from.

His wife. He let the words echo in his mind, liking the sounds of them. This time he'd go into marriage with his eyes open. None of that love business. Lydia had a few hang-ups about love, but she was intelligent, he'd help her see around them.

They were good partners. Excellent partners really, with the baby and the household. She made him more complete, he realized. Not only that, but they could keep Jasmine. He hadn't realized how much he cared for the baby until they'd been faced with letting her go.

If he kept the baby maybe he could keep Lydia too.

"It's not that simple," he said, both to the girl and himself.

"Tell me how it can be," she said, looking like the street tough he knew she had to be to survive in South Dade county. "Because a series of foster homes is not what I want for Jasmine."

"Do you have time to come with me to Family Services?"

"Yes."

Eleven

Lydia couldn't stand the wait a minute longer. The sheriff's office receptionist had told her Evan had asked for her to wait for him at home and that he would be home by five. Now it was almost six. Where the heck was he?

She realized it was cowardly, but she needed to get the baby to Evan so she could go home and lick her wounds in private. If her friends back home could see her now they wouldn't recognize her. She'd changed from the society lady who helped out from a distance, preferring to keep her hands clean by raising money for her charities instead of actually helping with them.

She hadn't known how much she was missing. Jasmine had opened her eyes to a whole new world, and

Lydia was glad of it. Even though her heart felt like it was breaking, she wouldn't have traded her time spent caring for the baby for anything in the world.

Her nose itched, and she felt like she was going to cry. She needed to keep it together. She didn't want to be sobbing in Evan's arms again. Besides, they hurt each other too badly when they tried to communicate at the gut level.

"Mamamama…ma…ma."

She jerked around and looked at the baby who was staring at her. She went to the playpen where Jasmine was surrounded by the toys she and Evan had purchased for her.

"Mama."

Her heart lurched, and she cuddled the baby close, breathing in her sweet scent and feeling that soft warm body close to her in her arms.

How she wished the baby was going to keep on being hers. Hers to care for and love. It was what she'd been searching for, she realized.

A home and family of her own.

Her father had awakened the need in her when he'd started pushing her to marry. Only, the right man wasn't in Manhattan. She'd had to drive hundreds of miles to find him.

"Oh, sweetie, I sure will miss you."

Someone cleared their throat, and she looked up into silver-gray eyes. Evan was back.

Something in the way he looked at her made her resolve crumble and she felt hot tears moving down her face. She grabbed Jasmine's blanket and wiped her eyes.

"I swore I wasn't going to do that today."

Evan walked into the living room, big and bold. He always moved with confidence, she realized and felt a sense of pride because he was her man. Whether he wanted to admit or not, the two of them had bonded in a deep and elemental way.

"Where have you been?" she asked, trying to pretend that everything was normal.

"Jasmine's mother showed up today."

Oh. The pipe dream she'd secretly harbored of her and Evan keeping the baby went up in smoke.

"She wants you and I to keep the baby."

Lydia was sure she'd misunderstood him. "Why?"

"She's been watching you with the child. She feels that you'll give her the love and care Jasmine needs and that I'll be able to protect Jasmine from the harsher parts of life."

"Can she give us the baby? Is that legal?"

"No. But I talked to Family Services, and they've agreed to let the baby stay with us in temporary care until I apply to adopt her."

"Oh, Evan, that's great."

He cleared his throat and came forward, staring at the baby in her arms and not at her. "I'd like for you to stay too, sugar. Stay and be a mother to this baby."

Lydia's heart melted at his words. They were the ones she'd been hoping to hear. Even though he'd said he didn't believe in love, she knew he had to care for her the same way she cared for him. She wanted them to be a family too.

She thought of her father and how he'd react when she called him and told him she'd found a man and was getting married. She knew in her heart that he'd be happy for her. After all, marrying her off was his first priority.

"What are you asking me to do? Live with you?"

"I'm asking you to marry me."

Yes, she thought and wanted to do a happy, Snoopy dance of joy. "I knew you wanted more than lust, but I didn't think you wanted love," she said.

As he watched her, all the happiness he'd been radiating dried up, and he stared at her as if she'd suddenly grown another head. An inkling of anxiety spread through her body, and she watched him, waiting for the other shoe to drop.

"What are you saying, Lydia?"

"That I love you."

"Ah, sugar…"

Gut instinct told her to stop talking, but she couldn't. She knew that it was now or never. She had to lay all her cards on the table. "You love me too, don't you?"

He touched her face, and Lydia felt the rough abrasion of his callused palm against her cheek. Loved the way he cupped her face in his hand and made her feel like she was cherished.

"No," he said.

She quivered, leaning against the back of the couch.

Shattered, she glanced down at her feet. Down at the hardwood floors that she'd covered with an Indian blanket she'd found in the craft shop at the women's center.

How could he touch her so tenderly, make love to her so deeply and not care about her?

Why had she said the words? They'd made her weaker than she'd ever been before. She'd given him the same weapon her father had owned. And her father had abused that love, she realized. It should have made her reluctant to love again, as she was sure Evan was. But it hadn't.

She wanted to call back her declaration, but it was too late. She couldn't. Besides, she saw the worry in his gaze.

"I told you how I feel about love."

"I could marry a wealthy man at home who doesn't love me."

"Is that what you're running from? A man who doesn't love you?"

"Yes."

"At least I care for you. I'm the only man you've let make love to you. That has to count for something, Lydia."

"Of course it does. You see, I'm not afraid of my emotions, and I can admit I love you."

How was she going to live with this? She needed to leave, to escape. But running away in the dark of night wasn't a solution this time. She needed to think.

"Then prove it and marry me."

"I can't," she said. Part of her wanted to take the risk and stay with him and Jasmine. It was what she wanted more than many things in the world, but not more than her own self-confidence. And living with a man who didn't love her would destroy her.

Evan felt like the tough hombre Eden wanted him to be to protect Jasmine from the cold hard world as he watched Lydia. He felt much the same as he had the first day at the FBI academy—desperately wanting something that he wasn't sure he'd get.

Lydia wore her designer clothing again instead of one of his shirts and a pair of cut-off jeans she'd gotten at the women's shelter. She looked like she was too good for the likes of him and, as he'd watched her draw into herself, he knew that she was.

Lydia deserved a big city and designer department stores. She deserved to go to theaters and symphony halls. He was blue jeans and beer and the annual rodeo. He wondered if he had the right to convince her to stay. To ask her to give up what she'd been looking for.

Hell, he knew there were men out there who would offer her love. They'd never appreciate her the way he did, but they'd give her those lying words she craved so desperately.

"I guess there's not much more to say on the subject of marriage. Tell me more about the process you need to go through to legally adopt Jasmine," she said.

"I'd rather finish our discussion."

"No, you wouldn't. Because I'm not feeling very nice right now." For the first time since he'd met her, she fairly vibrated with tension.

"It's okay. I can handle your anger."

"I can't," she said softly, clenching her hands at her sides, and he watched her battle with her own feelings.

It hurt him to realize he'd done this to her. But he still wanted her in his life. "Ah, sugar, please reconsider."

He pulled her close. The baby nestled between them. It felt right, he thought, to have his family in his arms and protect them both with his body. He knew that it was temporary, and that he couldn't really protect them from life. He wondered if that was why he didn't just say the words Lydia needed to stay.

"I could lie to you and say the words, Lydia."

She stepped out of his embrace and walked across the room. He watched her move away with none of the fluid grace she usually had, and felt like a big bastard. How was it that every time he came close to the gentler sex he managed to come away feeling like a hulking brute?

"You wouldn't lie," she said, meeting his gaze.

Of course he wouldn't. "Hell."

She set the baby back in her playpen and Jasmine crawled around until she found her stuffed lamb and then settled on her side with her thumb in her mouth. He'd come so close to having it all. She'd stay for three little words. Words that meant something deep and profound to her. Words that had ruined his life before.

It had taken time to get over Shanna, but he had, and he'd come out of it a stronger man. A man who'd looked hard at himself and his life and realized where he was going. And the path he was on now was a bumpy one, but it was his own path.

"I told you, love is a myth."

"I know. I thought I'd shown you otherwise."

"Ah, sugar. I know you want the words, but I care for you. More deeply than I've ever cared for a woman before, isn't that enough?"

She bit her lip. He had the idea that if he made love to her, he could convince her to stay. He wanted to reach for her, pull her into his arms and do whatever it took to break through the barrier she'd placed between them.

"No, it isn't enough. I settled once. I'm not going to again."

"It'll be different with me," he said, hoping he sounded confident and not desperate.

"We both deserve better, Evan. If I'm not the woman you love, then you should wait for her."

She walked out of the room, leaving behind the baby, the scent of her perfume and the man who ached to make her stay with him, but not at the price she wanted.

"Are you going to run away again, Lydia?" he taunted. Damn, he was mean sometimes.

"I'm not running."

Ah, hell. Her eyes were bright with tears again. All he ever did was make her cry.

"I don't want to hurt you, but I think we could have a happy life together."

"Without love."

"Yes, dammit."

"I want more."

"What would we have if I said the words that we don't have now?" he asked. He really wanted to know. Because for the life of him he couldn't see how three little words were going to change their lives.

"Mutual respect, deep affection...commitment."

"We have all those things now. At least I do."

She sighed. "I do too."

"Then what's the hang-up? Marry me."

He knew she was considering it. The baby had closed her eyes and was sleeping in her playpen. He pulled Lydia into his arms and kissed her. He took her mouth under his, and reminded her with his embrace of how good things were between them.

He tasted the coffee she'd drunk while waiting for him, and more than that, the essence of this woman. The one woman he needed to make his family complete. He thrust his tongue deep in her mouth and she moaned, wrapping her arms around him.

She wanted him too. Her grasp on him was strong and demanding, filled with feminine energy. He realized she was the yin to his yang. It was humbling.

"Will you do it?"

"Marry you?" she asked. He knew she was stalling for time.

He nodded. "Marry me."

"Yes... Evan, I'll marry you when you can love me."

"Lydia, love is a fool's game. Neither of us is a fool."

She walked away, stopping in the archway. "Then why do I feel like one?"

She left the room, and it felt as though she'd taken the life out with her. She'd thrown down the gauntlet. Big tough warrior that he was, all he could do was stare at it—afraid to leave it alone and afraid to pick it up.

Lydia heard the phone ring and Evan's heavy footsteps as he went into the den to answer it. She hurried back into the living room and scooped up the sleeping Jasmine. The baby would sleep better in her own crib.

It made her heart a little lighter to think of Jasmine growing up here on the Rockin' PJP. Payne would teach her all the things that old Florida cowboys had done for ages and the ranch hands would dote on her. And Evan, though he'd never admit it, would love her quietly and from a distance, protecting his heart for the day that Jasmine would be grown and leave the ranch.

Despite what he said, she knew love wasn't a fool's game, and Evan had to know it too. Why was he so afraid of three little words? Maybe he wasn't.

Maybe it wasn't that he couldn't love, but that he didn't love her. Why would he? She was on the run and hadn't even given him her real name. She wasn't someone who could stay here with him even if he did love her. Not until she put the past to rest.

She closed Jasmine's door, leaving it open just a crack, and went back downstairs, stopping on the bottom step. Evan stood in the doorway. In his uniform he bore little resemblance to the rebel who'd answered the door that first night wearing nothing more than a towel.

She felt dazed and confused. Unsure of her situation but not of herself. For the first time in her life she knew who Martine Lydia Kerr was. And she liked that woman.

"I have to go down to the station. We have a situation that only I can handle."

"Okay."

"It's not okay. I wanted to finish our discussion."

"Is that what you call it?"

"Yeah."

"I would have said we were arguing."

"Does it matter?"

"No."

She didn't have anything else to say without resorting to banal chatter, and they really didn't do that well. "Be careful, Evan."

He crossed to her, buried his hands in her hair and took her mouth in a kiss that was deeply carnal and deeply masculine. He claimed her with that kiss. She felt his mark left indelibly on her soul. She'd never be able to remember him and not think of that kiss. He pulled back before she could respond.

"Dammit, woman. Be here when I get back."

"I will. I'm not going to sneak away in the night. You'll know when I'm gone." Her days of running away were over.

"I didn't want this to happen," he said.

She knew her confusion showed on her face. "I never wanted to want you."

He didn't say anything, but turned on his boot heel, and walked away. She stood there after the door had closed and waited for her pulse to calm. She felt as if he'd lashed her to the bone.

They were doing too good a job of hurting one another she realized. Each of them wanted something the other couldn't provide, and neither of them knew how to back down. At least she didn't. She couldn't stay where she wasn't wanted and whether he admitted it or not, Evan didn't really want her here on any terms other than his own.

She wasn't content to stay within the boundaries he'd demand of her. Though she hadn't really entertained the notion of staying in a loveless marriage with him, she knew now that she never would. She knew in her heart that Evan wanted her, but he wanted her on his own terms and marriage or any partnership had to be give and take. It couldn't be all one-sided.

It was time to start preparing to leave, she thought. Jasmine had Evan and Evan would protect and cherish

the little girl. She knew how important that baby was
to him.

With resolve, she marched into the den and dialed
her father's home number. No more third-party mes-
sages. Their butler, Hammet, answered the phone on
the first ring. After a brief and somewhat cold discussion, she told her father where she'd been and that she
needed some money to get back home.

He agreed. And at the end of their conversation, just
before she hung up the phone, he said, "I love you,
baby."

"Daddy, I love you too."

She realized that her father loved her. Had really
known it all along, but it was so nice to talk to a man
who wasn't afraid of telling her his feelings. Tears
burned in her eyes again as she hung up the phone.

She turned to find Payne standing in the doorway.

"You're leaving?"

"Yes."

"I'd hoped you'd stay with my boy."

"Your boy doesn't really want me."

"I find that hard to believe."

"Well he'd like me to stay, but I need more."

"Marriage?"

"No, he offered that."

"What then?"

"Love."

Payne nodded. "The boy always has had problems
with it."

"Why?"

"I don't know. I think it has something to do with his mom dying when she did. He's never been able to talk about his feelings since that."

"Did he love his wife?"

"Yes. Sometimes I think she took his heart with her when he left."

"He's pining over her?"

"Never. But she left him like his mom did."

What Payne said made a lot of sense. She wished she knew how to break down the barrier that Evan had wrapped around his heart, but she didn't. She knew she'd stay if she thought there was a chance he'd come to love her, but he'd said love was a fool's game. And there had been absolute certainty in his voice.

Her money would arrive in the morning and she could leave. She'd have to find someone to watch Jasmine. Evan was going to have to go to work. She wanted the peace of mind of knowing her little family was taken care of, even if she wasn't the one caring for them. She missed them already, in a way she'd never missed her old life, and she hadn't even left.

Twelve

Lydia felt a little better after Charlotte had left that evening. She'd called her friend from the women's center and invited her over for dinner while Payne had joined the ranch hands in the bunkhouse. Due to Evan's schedule he was going to need baby-care coverage at hours other than the ones the Baptist Church offered. Lydia squashed her guilt at asking Charlotte to watch Jasmine before she'd told Evan she was leaving by justifying it as doing what was right for the baby.

She knew in her heart that he'd appreciate that she'd taken care of Jasmine first. She couldn't leave until she knew the baby was going to be well cared for during Evan's working hours. Charlotte had arranged

to have the next week off so that she could watch
Jasmine and help Evan find a reliable baby-care provider.

The house was quiet now. The full moon rose over
the empty horse pen. In the distance she heard the
lowing of the cattle and the random conversation of
ranch hands returning from a night on the town.

Evan still wasn't home, and it was almost midnight.
His job was demanding: he provided protection that
most people didn't even know was there, but took for
granted all the same. He was a special kind of man,
and it broke her heart that she was leaving him. But
she couldn't stay. A truck pulled into the driveway,
and she watched it make its way to the back door and
stop.

Evan was home. She hurried into bed, pulling the
covers up to her chin. How silly. It wasn't as if he
could have seen her in the window watching for him.

She heard his footsteps in the hall. Heard him open
the door to Jasmine's room, imagined him going in
and brushing a kiss on the baby's soft cheek.

Then the booted steps stopped outside her door. It
creaked as he opened it and walked into her room. She
knew she was leaving. Knew there was no point in
staying here with a man who couldn't love. But the
expression on Evan's face—part fierce—part angry
touched her. She realized she couldn't leave without
trying one last time to get through to him.

Maybe if she made love to him he'd understand the

depth of the feelings she had for him—and acknowledge the depth of his feelings for her.

She lifted the covers and scooted over to create a
space for him. He took off his boots, hat and belt and
then hesitated. He was always so self-assured that it
struck her, he was now as insecure with her as she
was with him.

"Come here and let me make love to you," she
said.

He finished removing his clothes and stood there in
the light cast by the moon. Totally male. Looking elemental in the primitive lighting. She skimmed her
eyes down his body, following the hair on his chest
that tapered to a thin line before his groin. He was
rock-hard, and she wanted to touch him. To pleasure
him the way he'd pleasured.

She rose on her knees and held out her hand. He
took a few tentative steps forward. Her blood began
pumping in a primal rhythm. She knew that this was
a mating dance. The most important dance a man and
a woman could do. The one that she and Evan had
needed for so long. Where she met him as an equal
and wasn't a passive participant.

He stopped in front of her, and she walked her fingers up his washboard stomach. His muscles quivered.

"Ticklish?"

"No," he said.

His voice brushed over her senses like a cool rain
on a summer's day, bringing unexpected pleasure. She
leaned forward and let her lips follow her fingers from

his stomach up to his neck, nibbling on him. He tasted warm and salty. She gently bit one of his nipples and heard his breath rasp between his teeth. She wanted to hear that sound again. Wanted to give to him in a way she'd never given to any other man.

"Lie down," she said.

He did.

"Bend your knees."

Again he followed her direction.

She rocked back on her heels and looked at him. He was magnificently male. She pulled her nightgown over her head and tossed it aside. Kneeling between his legs, she put her shoulders back and let him admire her, knowing he liked what he saw.

She leaned forward. "I want to know what you taste like."

"I want you to know."

She took him in her mouth, tasting the essence of man. His hands gripped her hair and fondled down her body to her nipples, pinching them lightly. His hands on her flesh always made her feel voluptuous. She moved under him, taking him deeper into her mouth.

He pulled her away. His touch roamed down her back and hips, and he plunged two fingers into the heart of her. She reared back on her legs to give him more access to her secrets. He urged her forward to straddle his hips, and their eyes met as she centered herself over his straining erection.

"Now?" she asked.

"Now."

He rocked upward and she slid down, impaling herself on him. He thrust deeper into her, and she felt as if he would touch her womb. He joined his hands and hers, holding her fiercely in his touch.

Her head fell to his shoulder and he bit her neck, sucking the spot to soothe it afterward. She felt her body tense everywhere. Electric tingles raced through her toward the finish. She lifted her head.

Their eyes met and held as their bodies moved faster to the promise of fulfillment waiting for them. Lydia tried to slow the pace, not wanting this moment to end, but couldn't.

Evan freed his hands and held her hips, controlling both her thrusts and his. The pace was frantic until everything inside her buckled and her womanly place clenched around him. He threw his head back, and with a loud groan, jetted to completion.

Lydia sank down on him, cradling him in her arms, knowing a contentment she'd never known before. Knowing a fracturing sense of intimacy and the truth that leaving wasn't going to be enough. She might never know the soul-shattering intimacy that she'd shared with Evan again. After what they'd shared, surely he'd be able to share his feelings with her.

"I love you," she said.

And his silence was all the answer she needed.

Evan crept out of bed the next morning, and Lydia rolled to her side feigning sleep. Tears burned the back of her eyes, and she knew she'd gambled on love and lost. She was glad that today she'd have the money to go home.

Lydia heard the door close quietly and sat up in the bed. As soon as he left for work, she'd pack and get on her own way. There was nothing holding her back now.

Jasmine cried out, and Lydia went across the hall to get the baby. Her little face was red as she cried for all she was worth. Her needs were the most important thing in the universe.

Lydia rocked and soothed her and, in the process, soothed herself. There was a big piece of her heart that would always belong to Evan Powell. But she knew that she'd still be able to love a child as much as she loved this little baby girl who'd taught her so much about herself.

She diapered the baby and took her downstairs to feed her her breakfast. Two empty cereal bowls sat in the sink and she knew that Evan and Payne must have already eaten. She fed the baby her peaches.

Someone knocked on the door. Propping Jasmine on her hip she hurried to see who was there.

She was surprised to see her father. He looked pale and out of breath but as elegant as ever in his three-piece suit. She was shocked to see Paul, her ex-fiancé. She'd hoped never to see him again after the embarrassing incident in his apartment.

"Hello," she greeted them. She was so happy to see her dad. She'd never realized how much she missed him. Unable to stop herself, she reached for him, hugging him with her free arm. He returned her embrace, holding her closer.

"Thank God, you're okay," her dad said.

"I'm sorry if I worried you. You look pale—how are you?"

"I'm fine. Or I will be when I get you back to New York."

"This is all very nice, but what is going on here, Lydia?" Paul asked. "And whose baby is that?"

"Let's go inside and discuss this," her father suggested.

"Yes, come in. Can I get you something to drink?"

Paul and her father shook their heads.

The men entered, and she seated them in the living room, hoping that Evan had gone to work and wasn't just out with his father doing the morning chores. This situation could get awkward.

Her father asked for the bathroom, and Lydia directed him to it. Jasmine was restless, so Lydia placed her in the playpen with her favorite toys. She hoped her disappearance hadn't affected her father's health.

"Well, isn't this a nice domestic scene? I hope you haven't become too attached to it," Paul said.

What if I have? she thought. "Why?"

"Because I'm not ready to be a father. I'm only marrying you to keep my career on track. I've worked too hard to let this chance slip away."

"Paul, I'm not marrying you. I told you that before I left."

"I flew down here with your father to prove I'm

the devoted fiancé. All you have to do is play your
part, and we will both get what we want. You don't
have a choice at this stage of the game.''

''Yes, she does,'' her father said from the door.

''Sir! I didn't mean it that way.''

''Yes, you did. And you're right. You have worked
hard for your promotion, but executives in my company have to be more considerate. We have a repu-
tation for being a company with a heart. Paul, I don't
know if you realize how important that is?''

''I can, sir.''

''Why don't you take the rental car back to the air-
port? We'll talk first thing Monday morning.''

Paul left quickly. Lydia faced her father, unsure
what to say. She'd been planning to battle with him if
need be to get him to see reason, but now he'd reached
that understanding on his own. And she didn't want
to fight him. Here was the love and support she
needed, especially when Evan refused to love her.

''Lydia, who's here?'' Evan asked from the kitchen.

''My father.''

Evan entered the room, and she watched the two
men she loved stare each other down. They were both
dominant men used to being in positions of power.

''Martin Kerr, meet Sheriff Evan Powell,'' Lydia
said.

Evan offered his hand to her father and, though the
whole event was civilized on the outside, she felt as
if she were watching two knights about to do battle
on a field of honor.

The tension in the room was thick. Lydia nervously twirled the sapphire ring her father had given her for her sixteenth birthday. She knew that she should say something to ease the strain, but words escaped her.

The only thing she could think of was that it was time to go, and that was the last thing she wanted to do. She searched Evan's face for some inkling that he felt the same way but saw nothing. His eyes were as cold as hard steel and his body language didn't bode well. She closed her heart to him, cut off all feeling because getting emotional was the last thing she wanted to do.

She went to Jasmine and picked her up, using the baby as her security blanket. Her father, who was an old pro at keeping conversations going, was questioning Evan about the running of the ranch, asking him if it was profitable and if they'd been affected by the Free Trade Agreement.

The old cowardly Lydia would have sneaked out of the room and upstairs. She would have brought her suitcases down this morning before getting the baby out of bed and been halfway home by now. But the new Lydia wasn't that meek and timid. The new Lydia knew that she deserved to be loved and to be happy. The new Lydia felt as if her heart was breaking and it would never be repaired.

"Well, Lydia, are you ready to go?" her father asked.

"Go?" Evan blurted.

"My running days are over. I'm going home," the new Lydia announced.

"What about Jasmine?"

"I've asked Charlotte to come and stay with her. She'll be here by 10:00 a.m."

Her father watched them both. There were words Lydia wished she could say to Evan but couldn't. Not now. Not after she'd bared her soul to him last night and received cold hard silence in return.

"Lydia, may I have a word with you in the other room?" Evan turned and walked through the door.

"Sure. Dad, will you watch Jasmine?"

Martin nodded. Lydia followed Evan out of the room. She prayed she'd be able to keep her emotions held tightly in check while she was alone with Evan. She realized there were disadvantages to loving someone and letting them know, not the least of which was that you had no defenses where they were concerned.

After last night, Evan had known Lydia wouldn't stay. There was a certain sadness in her body after she'd confessed her love to him and he'd been unable to respond. It wasn't that he felt nothing for her. Quite the opposite, he cared deeply for her, but that declaration was poison to a man.

The words were a myth that some believed in to the exclusion of all else, but they weren't enough to make a couple last forever. They never did. Love couldn't survive the mundane details of everyday life. Honesty, respect, affection: those were the hallmarks of a solid relationship.

He knew he couldn't ask Lydia to stay, but deep inside he wanted her to. They were both vulnerable where the other was concerned, and he sensed that Lydia lacked trust in him. He acknowledged that he'd always known deep inside that, despite her professed love, she would leave. She was the kind of woman who wouldn't be happy living in a small town and raising a family.

Though he knew she was justified in leaving, a part of him wondered how solid this "love" of hers was if she were willing to run home to daddy at the first opportunity. Her father appeared to be a rich, powerful man, confirming what Evan had suspected from the beginning—Lydia was out of his league.

This is what came of emotional entanglements, he thought. No matter how good it felt while he was making love to her, riding horseback over his family's land or watching Jasmine with her, he'd known it was temporary.

He knew better than to let Lydia close to him. Somehow she'd managed to sneak past his guard and now he had to pay the price. He'd been counting on the baby to make her stay.

"Your last name's not Martin?"

"Well, no...you knew I didn't give you my real name."

"Yeah, I did. Why are you running home to daddy now?" His words were unfair; she'd never committed to staying, but he was feeling like a matador gored by a bull after arrogantly assuming that the bull was docile.

"I'm not running anymore. I'm looking for a reason to stay," she said. Her voice was even and calm. Not raw as it had been last night.

He tried to imagine her in her big city. He realized he didn't even know where it was. "You think you'll find it in your father's home, wherever that is?"

"It's in Manhattan. Where my life is. You haven't given me reason to stay."

"Why did your dad show up today?"

"I called him for money. He must have traced the call."

"Why'd you decide to leave?" he asked.

"Jasmine needs you," he said. His heart echoed the words. *I need you.* But he wouldn't admit it out loud. He knew better than to say those words.

"Jasmine needs a mom, and I'd love to fill the bill. But any caring woman would right now."

Lydia's eyes were bright with tears, and he knew that leaving was hard for her. Why wouldn't she stay? Why did she have to be so stubborn? What they had was better than most couples ever found, why couldn't she see that?

"Only a special lady can take care of her. A lady willing to raise another person's child is unique, and I don't think any other woman cares as deeply for Jasmine as you do," he said softly.

"Jasmine is very important to me. I love her and

would like nothing better than to be her mother. But you are going to be her father, Evan. And I believe that parents should love each other.''

''Hell.''

She crossed to him, and her small hand cupped his face. The touch burned through him, bringing back all the white-hot memories of the night before, when she'd made love to him, bared her heart and soul to him. For her sake, he wished he still believed in love. If any woman deserved to be loved it was Lydia.

''Don't you see, Evan? It would eventually push us apart, because I need something you can't give me.''

''Three little words.''

''It's more than that.''

''Not from my point of view.''

''Then we have nothing more to say to each other.'' She pivoted and walked away.

''Don't go.'' The words were torn from deep inside him. He wanted to call them back as soon as they left his mouth.

''Give me a good reason to stay. Give me those three little words.''

Three little words.

He knew that if he said the right words to her she'd remain with him. But he couldn't say them. He'd given up on love a long time ago, and it was too late now to start believing in fairy tales.

''Be my wife.''

''Not those words, and not without love.''

She walked away, and anger boiled over in him.

Anger at her and himself. He'd watched her retreat so many times he should be used to it by now, but he wasn't. He hated to see her leave him again. He recalled the number of times she'd walked away without looking back. His gut tightened, and he let his emotions speak for him. "Running away isn't the solution, sugar."

She paused, glancing over her shoulder at him. "What is?"

"I don't know, but a real woman would stay and fight for her family."

The tears that had been threatening fell silently down her face, and she left without another word. He closed his heart to her face. Refused to acknowledge what he knew deep inside. He'd cut her to the bone and hit her where she was most vulnerable. Her father gave him a cold glare as he followed Lydia out of the house and out of his life.

He turned and kicked the wall next to the gun cabinet, putting his foot through it. Dammit to hell, he thought.

The house was quiet and empty. Even the baby was quiet, and he knew that his life had returned to the way it was before a sexy, cool blonde had disturbed his evening several weeks earlier. Too bad he couldn't go back to the man he was before, because that man didn't know what he'd been missing. Evan did.

Thirteen

Lydia and her father flew home in his private jet after making arrangements to have her car shipped to a mechanic in New York. Her dad looked pale and tired, taking Lydia's mind off her broken heart.

As soon as they reached cruising altitude, her father usually started working on his computer, phone and fax machine. His jet was decked out as a flying office. But today he sat pensively next to her.

"I'm sorry things didn't work out with Paul. He would have made you a good husband."

"What makes you think so, Dad? He didn't love me."

"Marriage isn't about love."

"Don't you wish you'd married mom?" she asked.

"She was my mate and the light in my heart, but marriages usually occur for business reasons."

"Not any more."

"More often than you think."

"Does my happiness matter to you?"

"More than my life," he said. The honesty in his eyes humbled her.

"Then let me stay unmarried until I find the man I can love."

"I need to know that you're settled in case something happens to me."

"What would happen, Dad?"

"I could die."

It was the first time he'd ever acknowledged he wasn't invincible, and that scared her. She moved across the aisle and sat in the plush chair next to his. "Someday."

He didn't reply.

"What's wrong?"

Again silence.

"Dad, I'll call Dr. Griffin as soon as we land. You know he'll tell me what your medical file says."

"He won't." After a long pause, he took her hand in his. "I'm dying."

Hearing him say what she'd suspected cut her to the bone. She realized that her father had been protecting her. "This is why you've been trying to marry me off?"

"Yes."

"Don't you think I would want to spend time with

you? What if something had happened while I'd been in Florida?''

"I had a private investigator searching for you. We were rather close to finding you." Her father was outwardly so calm, but there was a deep weariness in his eyes.

"What do you have?"

"Brain cancer."

Oh, God. "Can't you have chemotherapy?"

"It's too late to be effective."

"How much time did Dr. Griffin give you?"

"Six months from April fifteenth."

"But that's only a few more months."

"Honey, I'm not counting the days. I just want you to have someone in your life. I need to know that you're happy."

"You think a loveless arranged marriage would do that?"

"At least you'd have security, and the company would continue to be successful."

"Dad, I'm not marrying a man unless I love him."

"I think you've already found him."

"I thought so too."

"I heard what Evan said, sweetheart. He's right. You should have stayed with him."

"Without love, Dad? That's why I left Manhattan in the first place. I don't want a loveless marriage."

"Who said it would be?"

"He's never said he loved me."

"How has he acted?"

Evan had always treated her with respect and deep affection. He'd given her the security to try things she never would have attempted before, encouraged her to work in his community and to take charge of caring for Jasmine, showed her all that being his woman entailed, helped her put down roots.

"I thought he loved me. But he can't say the words."

"I never said them to your mother. I regret that now, but I felt they'd make me weaker somehow. As soon as I heard that her plane had crashed, the words echoed in my mind, but it was too late."

"What are you trying to say?"

"A strong man has different weaknesses. Ones that he might not admit to you or that you'd ever be able to see. But that man asked you to stay with him, honey."

"For the baby's sake."

"Do you honestly believe that's the only reason he wanted you to stay?"

Lydia thought about it. Her father was dying and life was short. She wasn't going to find another love in her life because what she felt for Evan was all-consuming and had been woven into the fiber of her soul. She'd left knowing she'd never love again, but now the situation had changed.

She knew she couldn't stay in Manhattan. There was nothing there for her. There never had been. She belonged in Placid Springs. She was a strong woman, she realized. Her father's daughter wouldn't docilely go home, she'd fight for her man.

"Dad, how would you feel about returning to Florida?"

Her father pushed the intercom button. "Charles, our plans have changed. Please take us back to Florida."

"Yes, sir."

Lydia smiled at her dad, and he reached over to hug her. For the first time in her life, she and her dad had communicated in a way that had always eluded them. "I love you, Dad."

"Love you too."

"I hope I can convince Evan to say those words."

"If any woman can, it's you."

The baby started crying as soon as Lydia and her dad drove away in their rented car. Evan scooped her up and looked down into her big brown eyes. "Well it's just me and you, kid."

"Drove her away, didya?"

Payne stood in the doorway. "She chose to leave."

"Why?"

"Because of three little words."

"Which ones?"

"Dad, we're not having this conversation. Can you watch Jasmine while I go change for work?"

"No."

"I thought you wanted grandkids."

"I want a daughter, too."

"It's not too late to marry the widow Jenkins. She's got three daughters."

"I had my mind set on Lydia."

"Well we're not really her kind of family."

"Oh, she turned snobby on you?"

"What?"

"I wouldn't have taken her for the kind to look down on hard-working folks like us."

"She didn't. She's used to a posh lifestyle, and I had no right to ask her to stay. It's a good thing she didn't."

Payne said nothing. Evan just watched his dad, listening to the silence in the room and in his house. His life was going to be cold and empty again.

"Dada…"

He looked down at little Jasmine. She'd legally be his daughter, but she already belonged to him in his heart. She wasn't the only person who lived there, he realized, Lydia was there too. Even though he'd been unable to say the words, he'd already known the truth.

He looked at the baby and faced his fears. Not admitting to loving Lydia hadn't made her leaving any easier on him. Watching her leave for the last time had brought home to him how very much she meant to him.

"Dad, I think I'm going to have to go to New York."

"Hot damn! I'll take care of the baby while you pack and book a flight."

"I don't even know where she lives."

"You'll find her. It's what you trained to do with the FBI."

"Never thought I'd use those skills again."

Lydia had her dad drop her off at the end of the driveway, and she walked toward the big ranch house. The journey that had been long and frightening that first night wasn't so bad now. Her dad was heading to Deerfield Beach to visit Aunt Gracie, who'd returned from Paris.

It had only been a few hours since she left, but it felt like a lifetime. She never wanted to be away from Evan and Jasmine for that long again.

She reached the front porch and Evan's dogs raced around the side of the house, circling her legs and licking her face when she bent to pet them. "At least someone's glad I'm back."

She stared at the big wooden door. Afraid to knock, but knowing this was it—her chance of a lifetime.

She climbed the steps quickly and knocked before she could change her mind.

There was no heavy sound of footsteps, but the door swung open and Evan stood there, chest bare and glistening with drops of water, a towel around his waist.

"Lydia."

Just her name. She wondered if he didn't believe she was standing there. She knew she couldn't fathom it. It took all her courage not to turn around and run back up the long driveway. She wasn't sure she could handle being rejected again.

"Evan."

"You came back."

"I decided you were right. I'm here to fight for my family. I'm not leaving again."

"You don't have to fight for us."

Was she too late? "I'm not going back to New York."

"Yes, you are."

"No. I'm not."

"But you belong there."

"I belong with you, Evan."

"Really, sugar?"

"Yes. And I'm going to convince you that saying three little words isn't going to make you weaker."

"Even though they've been unsaid they haven't gone unfelt."

"What are you saying?" she asked.

He mumbled something.

She stepped closer, her heart lighter. "Say it again."

"I...love...you," he whispered.

Lydia smiled and her heart felt full of joy. Evan pulled her into a bear hug that was so strong she couldn't breathe. He brushed his lips against her forehead, her cheek and finally her mouth.

His mouth consumed hers and she caressed his bare shoulders and chest.

"I love you too."

"I don't think I'm the kind of man who can say those words all the time, but I definitely feel them."

"What changed your mind?"

"Your leaving. I'd been saying I didn't love you because you were only here temporarily, but it didn't matter. I felt like an empty shell when you left."

"Where's Jasmine?"

"With my dad, at the cattle auction."

"So we're all alone?"

Evan swept her up in his arms and carried her up the stairs. Lydia knew she'd found the love she'd been searching for and the place where she belonged. And she'd found them both in the same man.

Epilogue

A year later, Evan and Lydia welcomed their firstborn into the world. Lydia's father and Payne were both in the waiting room when she'd given birth to Andy. Jasmine wasn't too sure of the newcomer and clung to Evan. He'd assured Jasmine that he and Mommy had enough love for both the new baby and their precious angel.

Evan had found that the love words he didn't think he'd be able to say came easier and easier. It helped that Lydia showered him with her affection all the time. She worked three days a week at the women's center, and everyone in town had been stopping by to see her and pat her belly as her pregnancy progressed. When she'd confessed to being uncomfortable with everyone knowing every detail of their lives, Evan had offered to move back to Manhattan with her. But she'd said she could never live anywhere else.

Martin was pale and gaunt but still holding his own. Evan had spent the last three nights being beaten at chess by Lydia's father. Martin had outwitted the doctors by living this last year, but they all knew it wouldn't be much longer.

Evan would miss the tough old guy. He couldn't help but be thankful that Martin had tried to buy his daughter a husband, scaring her away from the safety of her life in the city and straight into his heart.

* * * * *

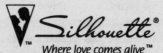

SILHOUETTE®
MAKES YOU
A STAR!

Look in the back pages of
all June Silhouette series books to find an
exciting new contest with fabulous prizes!
Available exclusively through Silhouette.

Don't miss it!

Silhouette®

Where love comes alive™

P.S. Watch for details on how you can meet
your favorite Silhouette author.

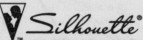